THE SPIDER:
THE DEVIL'S CANDLESTICKS

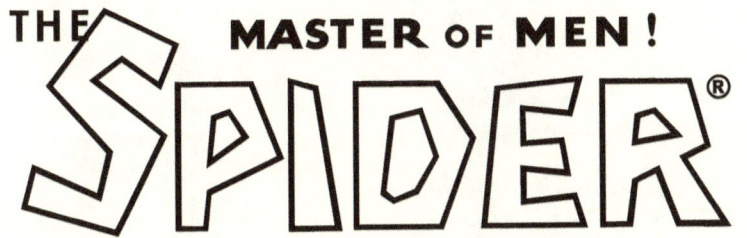

THE SPIDER

MASTER OF MEN!

THE DEVIL'S CANDLESTICKS

By Grant Stockbridge

POPULAR PUBLICATIONS • 2022

CHAPTER 1
GUILTY AS CHARGED

SOMETHING WAS very wrong. Richard Wentworth was certain of it the moment he put the telephone instrument back into its cradle and stared thoughtfully out over the East River flowing placidly beneath his windows. His keen blue-gray eyes narrowed slightly, and his flat-planed vital face became harder, more sharply etched, as he endeavored to puzzle out the real trouble.

There had been nothing unusual about his being summoned downtown for a consultation in the offices of his brokers. But old Stuart Johnson's voice had been tinged with something that reached out and gripped at Wentworth's sensibilities—sounding a warning note in his brain.

"Dick, I—I'd like you to come down here as quickly as you can." The broker's queerly strained voice still rang in Wentworth's ears, tingling his nerves, oddly. "Something has happened—something that I can't discuss over the phone. Please... if you can come immediately...."

It was not fear that had made Johnson's voice sound so different, so suddenly changed. No, it was something beyond fear. It began where fear stopped—the appalling realization of inconceivable calamity. It was defeat, despair—the utter desperation so prevalent on the Street in those dark days of nearly ten years ago when the bottom had dropped completely out of the market.

Johnson's tone was that of a man who has received some sinister final summons and knows his time has come....

When Richard Wentworth strode into the brokerage office, twenty minutes later, the usually sprightly old gentleman behind the wide, flat-topped desk appeared exactly that—a doomed man with one foot already in the grave. Johnson had aged incredibly, and looked as if he had not slept for days. Deep lines showed in his face, a haggard look haunted his eyes, and a listless droop to his shoulders spelled overwhelming tragedy.

"We are finished, Dick." His gray head nodded slowly, almost

The hushed silence was followed by the shrieks of dying men and women.

mechanically, when Wentworth sat down beside his desk. "Crosby and Johnson are washed up—bankrupt—and our best customers are wiped out!"

The man seemed stunned, as if incredulously listening to his own words, forcing himself to understand that they were true.

"But my account isn't a speculative one." Wentworth's brows arched in surprise. "I haven't anything on margin. Crosby has been handling nothing for me but solid securities—"

"That's it—Crosby." Johnson nodded dazedly. "Crosby cleaned out your account, Dick—robbed you of fifty thousand dollars—and you are only one of a dozen of our customers." As he read the amazement in Wentworth's deep-set eyes, he went on: "I know it is unbelievable—but it's true. God Almighty. I *couldn't* believe it at first. Then I did everything I could to salvage the wreckage. I threw every dollar I own into the market. But when I learned the full extent of Crosby's defalcations, I knew that it was useless—what I could do wasn't a drop in the bucket."

His chin sank. "This morning I could protect him no longer, and Crosby gave up. He surrendered to the district attorney and confessed to misappropriating nearly a half million dollars. He admits it, Dick—but he makes *no* effort to explain why he did it, no attempt to justify himself. He merely sits there and looks straight ahead of him, as if in a trance. He just says, 'I did it, and that's all there is to it.' In all my years of acquaintance with Gilbert Crosby I never saw such a look on his face—"

But it was Johnson's face that Richard Wentworth was watching. In the broker's harried eyes, he saw nameless fear dawning—fear of the unknown that reached out and clutched him terrifyingly. Into Johnson's mind, he knew, had flashed the same thoughts that were in his own.

"What is this thing that is coming over people, Dick?" Stuart Johnson put the terror into words. "Men I have known for years—men who were the very epitome of honor and integrity—they all seem to have gone utterly mad! Raoul Whittaker—a man of his caliber to rob the institution trust fund in his care! Morton Stevenson—who ever would have believed that he would deliberately swindle jewelers out of a quarter million dollars worth of precious stones? Hugh Delaney—he loved his niece more than anyone in the world, yet he stole every penny of the inheritance he was administering for her. Things like this aren't natural, Dick—any more than it was natural for Gilbert Crosby to turn thief."

"Gilbert Crosby is no thief." The words sprang involuntarily to Wentworth's lips, as he leaped to the defense of the man he had known all his life. "I don't care what he did or what he says he did...."

Suddenly, he stopped. A clammy chill crept through his veins, as he thought of those others Johnson had mentioned—as well as that multitude who had admitted to incredible crimes and made no attempt to defend themselves....

"Where is Crosby now?" Wentworth snapped the question.

"Police headquarters—in a cell, I guess," Johnson muttered. "He would not even let me arrange his bail."

"That's where we're going—as quick as we can get there." Wentworth was already on his feet, striding to the door and holding it open for the broker. "I want to talk to Crosby—before it's too late."

The last was little more than a whisper, but Stuart Johnson heard it and his haggard face turned a sickly, ashen white. Into his mind flashed the memory of friends whose amazing crimes had been no greater than Gilbert Crosby—and who had atoned in their own way before the law could pillory them farther. He fairly ran in his eagerness to keep up with Wentworth's lithe, vigorous stride.

A TAXICAB sped them to police headquarters, where Richard Wentworth's name quickly gained them admittance to the commissioner's office. Stanley Kirkpatrick was seated at his desk, a handsome, dignified man in his late forties, indelibly stamped with the mark of authority which comes from years of command. He glanced up expectantly. Then the half-smile on his florid, saturnine face faded as he glimpsed Stuart Johnson.

"We came to see you about Gilbert Crosby, Commissioner," Wentworth told him quickly. "Can we see him?"

"He is in the Tombs." Kirkpatrick's frown deepened. "Why are you interested, Dick—you one of the victims he trimmed?"

"Crosby and Johnson are my brokers," Wentworth nodded. "I have no complaint, but I'd like to see him. I want to know that he *can* see anyone, Commissioner—that's why I came straight to you."

Kirkpatrick caught the significance of that emphasis, and his shrewd eyes narrowed. Reaching for his desk phone, he called the Tombs office, asked about Gilbert Crosby—and sat staring thoughtfully at Wentworth as he waited long minutes for a reply.

"What?" the word suddenly exploded from his lips as he bounced upright in his chair. "Are you sure? When did that happen? Never mind—I'll be right over."

Dropping the receiver back into its holder, Kirkpatrick pushed back from his desk and looked straight at Wentworth, nodded an answer to the question in the eyes that steadily returned his stare.

"Too late," he admitted. "He's dead. Committed suicide in his cell. I'm going over to have a look at him. Coming along?"

Wentworth was on his feet, but Stuart Johnson sat in his chair like a graven image, every bit of color drained from his thin face.

"Dead," he repeated the word in a tone that was sepulchral. "A suicide like Whittaker... like Delaney... like John Blanchard. No... no, I don't want to see him!" He fairly cringed into his seat, as if he would glue himself to it.

Commissioner Kirkpatrick and Wentworth were already through the doorway, hurrying to the corridor that led to the Bridge of Sighs. A doctor and several keepers were gathered in Crosby's cell, when they reached it, but a single glance at the distorted face of the broker told them that no further examination was necessary. Gilbert Crosby was dead, features still twisted in the agony of the final convulsions.

"I ordered him searched thoroughly," Kirkpatrick snapped angrily.

"We did—we went over him with a fine-tooth comb," one of the guards defended. "I'd have sworn there was nothing on him."

"Nothing but a dose of sure-fire poison," Kirkpatrick muttered as he turned away and started back to the office. "He had it skillfully concealed, came prepared to kill himself at the first opportunity—just like the others. That makes four prisoners we have lost here in the Tombs—and at least six other suicides who did not wait to be arrested and brought here. All were people from the very best families—that's the part that gets me: why people like that should suddenly resort to crime. One who makes a slip, we can understand—but when our best people start going wrong by the dozens!"

"Gilbert Crosby was no crook," Wentworth insisted firmly.

"Neither was Whittaker or Delaney or Steven Bolton," Kirkpatrick agreed wearily. "Certainly, Celia Winant had none of the earmarks of a thief, and you would never pick Virginia Palmer for a swindler. They were all people we knew and liked—friends with whom we mingled regularly. Then suddenly they went haywire. Suddenly, they admitted to astounding crimes and made no attempt to explain or defend themselves—no answer except a bullet or a dose of poison." He shook his head.

"It isn't natural, Dick," he went on. "I have dealt with crime waves galore. Every time you find the perpetrators of crime merely weak-minded crooks. Either they are imitating someone who appeared to get away with it, or they are organized and directed by a will and brain stronger than their own. But

when our best people—college-trained men and women of wealth and position—suddenly go in for a crime wave, it doesn't make sense. It almost seems as if they *can't* know what they are doing, as if they are hypnotized into these confessions—like the political prisoners on trial in Russia!"

They had returned to the commissioner's office, where Stuart Johnson still cowered nervously. Wentworth faced Kirkpatrick across the desk over which they had met so many other challenges to society—and strangely that clammy chill again crept up his back. Fighting the lawless onslaughts of the Underworld was one thing, but when one's friends and intimates suddenly became criminal madmen without the slightest warning....

Kirkpatrick's telephone interrupted his puzzled groping. He reached for it—and again his eyes widened. He sat bolt upright with surprise as he clipped answers into the mouthpiece.

"More of the same," he turned to Wentworth as soon as the conversation ended. "The Standard Investment Corporation—"

"That's Bruce Fletcher's outfit," Wentworth nodded.

"He's dead—he and his whole board of directors!" Kirkpatrick clipped, as he led the way downstairs to a waiting police car. "It sounds preposterous—but Hamilton Taylor is being held for murdering them!"

THE SUMPTUOUS offices of the Standard Investment Corporation were crowded with uniformed officers and detectives when Kirkpatrick led the way through the door. Three ambulance interns had answered the hurry call for medical aid, but they were preparing to leave. There was nothing they could do—nobody could do anything, except the medical examiner and the undertaker.

Kirkpatrick pushed open the door of the board room, and stared at the council of corpses still slumped and sprawled in their chairs around the long mahogany table. Bruce Fletcher and eight of his directors. The only one absent was Hamilton Taylor, the vice-president—and he sat in the room beyond, white-faced, tight-lipped, ringed in by a dozen homicide squad men whose questions he ignored.

"He was caught dead to rights, Commissioner," a detective lieutenant confided to Kirkpatrick. "His secretary was suspicious—realized this fellow had been playing with the books, was watching him. Today Taylor tried to get the secretary into the board room here with the others. But Miller—that's the secretary—went in one door and out the other. It saved his life."

He explained. "Miller caught Taylor squirting poison gas through the keyhole, but by that time it was too late. When the first radio car got here, everyone was dead. Taylor played innocent, until Miller faced him—then he came through. Far as we can make out from Miller, Taylor's into the company for a couple hundred grand."

Wentworth stared at the badgered Taylor. He remembered the last time he had rubbed shoulders with the man in one of the city's most exclusive clubs. A member of an old, aristocratic family, Hamilton Taylor had always been regarded as scrupulously honest and beyond reproach—and now he sat here an admitted thief and murderer.

Kirkpatrick's saturnine features were even more grim than usual, as he regarded this man who had been one of his friends. He stared down unbelievingly into the expressionless face. The first knuckle of Kirkpatrick's right hand brushed back and forth against his spike mustache. Wentworth recognized from the familiar gesture how badly the commissioner was worried.

"What is this all about, Taylor?" Kirkpatrick demanded. "What have you to say for yourself—nothing?"

"Nothing, Commissioner." Hamilton Taylor nodded calmly. "Miller has said all that is necessary. There is nothing more I need add. These men are wasting their time questioning me."

"But you realize that this means you are facing the electric chair?" Kirkpatrick pressed patiently, as if trying to reason with a child. "You understand what it will mean to your family?"

Hamilton Taylor's face became stonier than ever, but his jaws were clamped together as if hewn from granite.

Silence followed.

"You know…" Kirkpatrick began again, but at that moment the office door opened, and a sergeant poked his head inside.

"There's a telephone call for you, Commissioner," he announced. "A call for you and Mr. Wentworth—they put it through from headquarters."

"Not for me—for you, Dick." Kirkpatrick handed over the instrument, as soon as he had spoken into it. "It's Nita."

Nita van Sloan—trying so persistently to reach him! That

meant trouble Wentworth knew even before he put the receiver to his ear.

"I've been trying to locate you everywhere, Dick," the voice that never failed to thrill him came over the wire, but now Nita van Sloan's rich contralto was vibrant with anxiety and excitement. "I am at home. I need you as soon as you can get here—you and Stanley. I'm glad he is with you. That may be just the help we need."

Wentworth knew Nita far too well to question the urgency of her call. They had been through so much danger together, so many spots where life itself hung on quick thinking and understanding, that frequently their association seemed almost telepathic.

Commissioner Kirkpatrick's response was equally swift.

"There is nothing more here," he said, the moment he heard her message, "and Nita may have the lead we need."

With screaming siren, the police car sped uptown to Riverside Drive while the two men on its rear seat silently wondered what awaited them. Instinctively, they sensed that whatever troubled Nita van Sloan was connected with this mysterious wave of baffling crime that seemed to be undermining New York society. Though neither would admit it, in the mind of each lurked a half-formed fear, a vague dread that the tentacles of the insidious evil had already reached out to engulf Nita....

NITA MET them at the door of her apartment. "It's about Grace Morrell," she told them quickly, her violet eyes dark with alarm. "I have her here with me now—and she seems to be in desperate trouble. When she arrived she was nearly hysterical.

She kept raving about having killed Judson. I couldn't quiet her until I made her take a sedative."

Grace Morrell was one of Hamilton Taylor's daughters. Wentworth's mind leaped at that significance. One of Taylor's daughters and one of Nita's best friends. Judson Morrell was her husband, and she had raved about having killed him!

Nita softly opened the door to a bedroom, looked in to see whether the girl was sleeping. Suddenly, she tensed in the doorway, eyes wide, mouth half-open as if the scream that welled up into her throat choked and would not come forth. Instantly, Wentworth leaped to her side, drew her back so that she would be out of the range of possible fire... then he saw what had frozen her into immobility.

Grace Morrell was no longer on the bed that still bore the indentation of her body. She had gone to the casement window, climbed up onto the sill and crawled halfway out onto the stone ledge. Too late to shout warning or plea, Wentworth hurled himself across the room, leaped to the sill—just as the girl flung herself headlong!

For a fraction of a second, he stood there, aghast, while her voice trickled back to him in a faint, wind-blown scream. Then he whirled, his poker face a bleak mask. He took Nita in his arms and led her away from the open window and the ghastly sight now sprawling horribly on the pavement far below.

Once more the grisly terror had lashed out swiftly and inexplicably, snatched a victim from the fullness of life and plunged her down to self-destruction. The fleeting glimpse of Grace

Morrell's despair-ridden face had stabbed into Richard Wentworth's great heart, echoing there the call to battle!

Three times within as many hours the devils who were behind this mystifying scourge had struck with impunity—then snapped the whip to cover their criminal tracks with the silence of sealed lips. So fiendishly successful had been those tactics that Kirkpatrick and his men were running around in circles, groping blindly for the smallest clue, while the terror spread like wildfire.

It was a challenge the Spider could not ignore—a challenge which he, alone, could meet. As he looked down into Nita's horrified eyes, angry blood pounded in his veins, and his fingers itched to come to grips with this cowardly menace that struck at helpless men and women and turned them into such desperate criminals!

CHAPTER 2
ANTEROOM TO HELL

"**W**HAT WAS that you said about Grace Morrell having killed someone?" Kirkpatrick pressed as soon as Nita had recovered her composure. Accustomed as he was to horror, the commissioner was pale.

"Judson—her husband." Nita's voice came shakily, as she tried to reconstruct the scene. "She was crying when she came in—I could hardly understand her. She kept repeating that Judson was dead, that she hadn't meant to kill him… then there was something about not being able to help herself, but having

to do what she was told. It
was all so hysterical that I
could hardly understand
the words, much less what
she meant. I hoped she'd
talk more lucidly, after her
nerves were calmed… but
now she will never speak
again. Oh, I shouldn't have
left her!"

"You could have done nothing," Wentworth assured her
bitterly. "If she had not managed to kill herself this way, she
would have found another. And the moment she became ratio-
nal her lips would have been sealed so that no power on earth
could unlock them. But she may speak yet—if we can find
Judson's body and learn how he died."

Nita did not know where the supposed killing had taken
place, but the Morrell apartment was the first place they investigated—and there they found him.

Judson Morrell lay on the floor in front of the open wall safe
in his living-room. A bullet from a pearl-handled revolver had
lodged in his heart, bringing almost instant death. On the floor
beside the safe lay the weapon and scattered around it were half
a dozen pieces of sparkling and expensive-looking jewelry.

Kirkpatrick examined them closely. "Paste," he decreed.
"Nothing but junk."

"But here are the originals," Wentworth added, as he opened
Grace Morrell's bag, lying on the table, and drew out exact repli-

15

cas of the pieces in Kirkpatrick's hands. "These are no junk—worth more than a hundred thousand dollars, I should say. Besides these securities," as he brought out an envelope filled with crisp certificates. "For some reason, Grace Morrell was looting her own safe, substituting those paste imitations for her jewels—when Judson came in and surprised her. They must have struggled, as he tried to stop her. In the scuffle, he was killed."

"But why?" Nita gasped. "She was devoted to Judson—I know that. Why was she robbing herself, and so desperate to conceal from him what she was doing, that she threatened him with a gun? I can't understand...."

"If I could answer that, I could tell you why people with whom we dine and go to the theater one night turn out to be confessed thieves and murderers the next," Kirkpatrick grumbled. "You said something about her not being able to help herself—but having to do what she was told. That means she was protecting somebody, trying to cover up for somebody else. That's the answer in her father's case, too. He won't say a word because he is desperately anxious to protect somebody else. But who can that be—"

"Perhaps Mildred—Grace's sister," Nita suggested, and the commissioner's face brightened.

Quickly, he dialed the Taylor home. But as Kirkpatrick listened to the voice over the wire, satisfaction faded from his countenance. His features became stern and hard.

"Mildred's gone," he said grimly. "Disappeared more than twenty-four hours ago, and has not been heard from since. There's our answer! Mildred Taylor was kidnaped, and her father and sister were desperate to ransom her. They had to get money no matter how—even though it meant robbery and even murder. If we can lay hands on the kidnapers who are holding her, we'll put an end to this wave of crime that now seems so inexplicable. These people we know so well—are not criminals. They have been driven to crime only to protect their loved ones—relatives snatched and held as hostages. Working with the Underworld crooks who are preying upon them, you will find someone we all know well—some society wastrel who keeps his pockets lined with cash by putting the finger on his friends."

That was a theory Kirkpatrick's chief of detectives had offered the newspapermen, Wentworth remembered. The police were blaming most of these society crimes on the "cafe set," and making life miserable for the night-club owners. But to Wentworth that theory was none too convincing. Somehow, these crimes did not have the Underworld flavor....

Yet, if Kirkpatrick was correct, Gilbert Crosby must have been trying to protect somebody when he robbed his customers and then committed suicide to seal his own lips. Trying to protect whom? His own family—his wife, or his young daughter Anice? If Kirkpatrick was right, Anice Crosby might be in grave danger at that very moment.

At least that was a lead, and Wentworth decided to investigate it.

"I shall be busy the rest of the evening, darling," he told Nita when he took her home to the Riverside Towers.

For a moment she looked deep into his eyes. Her hands gripped his arms, worked up to his shoulders and clutched them

RICHARD
WENTWORTH ·

as if she would hold him here with her. For a moment, her lips parted as if to voice a quick protest—then closed soundlessly.

Nita van Sloan knew how he would be "busy." As she looked deep into his stern eyes, she knew that one of those moments she dreaded was at hand. It was the moment when she must hand Richard Wentworth over to the Spider—watch him stride forth to match his wits and stake his life against the ruthless enemies of society who laughed at the law and feared nothing so much as the ebon-cloaked Nemesis who took their trail relentlessly when ordinary police methods failed.

Perhaps she could have held him here with her; perhaps he would have yielded to her pleas had she voiced them. But Nita van Sloan knew her man so well that she realized there could be no happiness for him in such forced retirement. So long as red blood pounded in his veins, and his blue-gray eyes became steel-hard at the spectacle of helpless men and women under the heel of a criminal oppressor—just so long must she release him to continue his shadowy patrol of the highways and byways of crime, to mete out impartial justice to those whom Society could reach in no other way.

"Be careful, Dick," she whispered, as he held her close and

pressed his lips against hers fervently. "Call me as soon as you can."

And then he was gone and she closed her door to face the lonely, anxious hours that seemed to be her lot in life. A lump began to rise uncomfortably in her throat and her eyes were smarting. Then resolutely she threw off such thoughts.

No matter how she might be able to change him, she admitted to herself, she wanted Richard Wentworth no different than he was. In that moment, a fierce pride in him welled up into her heart. He was a man in a million—her man. What more could she ask than a chance to help him by her silent coöperation, and by her active participation whenever chance gave her that opportunity?

MUCH THE same thoughts were in Wentworth's mind as he taxied across town to the Crosby home. Well he knew the ordeal to which he submitted Nita by these nocturnal prowlings, and appreciated the loyalty and devotion she so generously bestowed upon him. Some day he would be able to devote the rest of his life to rewarding her with the home for which she yearned, the husband she deserved, the youngsters….

But when that day came the Spider must be no more—and tonight the Spider had work to do that brushed everything else from mind the moment he stepped out of the cab.

The Crosby butler answered his ring, and ushered him into the presence of the grieving widow and her daughter. Elizabeth Crosby, whose word for many years had been law in the circles of New York's Four Hundred, was a distinguished-looking, well preserved matron in her early fifties. Her eyes were tear-dimmed and she retained her composure only with obvious effort. But she thanked Wentworth for his call and listened carefully to his questions.

"I fear I can't help you, Mr. Wentworth." She shook her head regretfully. "This tragedy came entirely without warning. I had not the slightest suspicion that anything was wrong. If Mr. Crosby had received any threats—if he was worried about any of us—he told me nothing."

"And you, Anice—" Wentworth swung suddenly to the daughter—"you had no inkling that anything was wrong? No idea what was worrying your father or who might have been pressing him?"

For an instant, the girl's pretty face blanched, blue eyes widened. She had been caught off-guard, and Wentworth read the panic in their depths. But she quickly regained her control.

"None whatever." Her head shook positively. "Father never spoke to me about matters of that sort."

Wentworth looked straight into her eyes, and was certain that she was lying, concealing something from him. But she had inherited Gilbert Crosby's firm chin and square jaw, and he knew that it would be useless to contradict her. Mrs. Crosby might be in ignorance of what had been going on, but Anice *knew*—and was not talking… Why, Wentworth didn't know.

SEVERAL POSSIBLE answers to that question ran through Wentworth's mind, as he walked through the doorway of the old mansion and started across the slightly sunken courtyard toward the short flight of steps to the street level. But before he reached those steps, a figure came catapulting at him soundlessly from the darkness. Wentworth caught only a partial glimpse of a shadowy form. Instinctively, he threw himself into a half-crouch. Then the fellow was on his back, clutching him with one arm while the other fist pounded away at his face.

For a moment, Wentworth had all he could do to protect his features, as he tried to tear the fellow loose from his shoulders. That did not work—until suddenly he heaved himself forward and pitched head over heels on the stone-paved court. It dislodged his assailant, and, before the fellow could get back on his feet, Wentworth was ready for him—meeting him with a jolting uppercut followed in quick succession by punishing pile-driving blows to the midriff.

The young fellow's mouth gasped open, but he gamely fought back the groan almost wrenched from him. About twenty-five, Wentworth judged—a chap of obvious refinement, but one he did not know. Deliberately, Wentworth set himself for the one-two that would be a merciful knockout. But before he could land the second blow, something came down with crushing force on the top of his head—a treacherous blow from behind!

Wentworth went down with the blow sufficiently to avoid being knocked unconscious. Dazedly, he dropped to his hands and knees, then rolled over on his back just as a figure bent over him with what looked like a piece of lead pipe. Wentworth steeled himself for the blow. But his assailant merely crouched there above him, while the young fellow, with whom he had been battling, leaped up the steps and dashed to a coupé standing at the curb. A starter whirred, the snort of a motor sprang into life—and then the car was speeding down the block.

Wentworth feigned uncon-
sciousness. But his slitted eyes
were glued on that dark figure
above him, his muscles tensed for
a desperate struggle should that
bludgeon raise again. Yet now
that the car had sprung away from
the curb, the fellow straightened
and cat-footed toward the steps…
directly across a beam of light that
Wentworth was watching like a
hawk.

It fell full on the man's face, for a fraction of a second—to
reveal a countenance that any theatergoer would have recognized at once. It was Preston Kendall, the internationally known
actor now starring on Broadway in *The Green Goddess!*

Preston Kendall… Wentworth rose slowly to his feet and
stepped to the edge of the court. His assailant was just rounding the corner. Preston Kendall—what could he be doing there
prowling in the darkness outside the Crosby home? It didn't
make sense, unless Kendall, too, had been bitten by this criminal
phobia that seemed to claim its victims from the most surpris-
ing sources—or unless Wentworth had been mistaken in the
man's identity.

There was one quick way to check on this. Walking to the
corner, Wentworth hailed a cab and was driven to the Continental Theater. The performance of *The Green Goddess* was already
in its last act. He bribed his way past the doorman and stood

at the rear of the orchestra long enough to witness Kendall's next entrance—to assure himself that the man in the role of the Indian prince was *not* Preston Kendall but an understudy!

So he had not been mistaken—it was Preston Kendall who had tried to split his skull....

But who was the young fellow who had started the attack? Wentworth recalled Stanley Kirkpatrick's theory that these

Knives streaked at that
midnight-hued figure, and
guns blazed at him!

mystifying crimes could all be traced to some young society
playboy who was preying on his friends and acquaintances.
That might be the explanation. Some nightclub habitué, the

commissioner had declared—and that might be the place to locate the fiend now.

Next to the Continental Theater was the Armageddon Club, one of the most fashionable in the city, operated by John Petrillo, whom the nightclub men had elected as an overseer of their business—a local czar to keep their places in good repute and combat the police campaign against them. Wentworth went into the place and found a table from which he could study the crowd. Fashionable and orderly, they seemed to be—nice people all of them. Petrillo, square-shouldered, well set-up, olive-skinned and suave, was the perfect host, his watchful eyes missing nothing that transpired in the big room.

From the Armageddon, Wentworth went to another fashionable night-club—to half a dozen of them in succession. But he saw no sign of his young assailant, and nothing that appeared in any way suspicious… significant, until he walked into Carlo Maggi's Savoy Club.

His man was not among the merry-makers there, but another of the guests brought Wentworth up short. Sitting at a table with one of Maggi's attractive entertainers was Allen Crosby, son of the man who had that day killed himself in the Tombs! **YOUNG CROSBY** seemed entirely sober, Wentworth noted. There was nothing foggy-eyed about him. In fact, he seemed keen, alert—as if nervously waiting for something to happen. Quickly, Wentworth's eyes traveled over the other guests in the place. Many were socialites whom he knew by name and sight. Others were well known Broadway figures—like Gooja Singh, the lavishly dressed Hindu aristocrat reputed to be something of a mystic, or Phil Deming, whose race-track killings were regular gossip-column items.

But a strange figure in that place was stern, austere-looking Milo Spencer, sworn foe of spiritualists, soothsayers, fortune-tellers, crystal-gazers and all of their ilk—a stiff-necked, puritanical crusader. Yet here he was among these early morning revelers.

And at the table behind him was Preston Kendall! Kendall, alert and watchful, giving only superficial attention to the chatter of his female companion while his eyes darted repeatedly toward young Crosby!

Wentworth felt his pulses quicken. Unobtrusively, he worked his way closer to Kendall's table. Then there was an interruption that caused a stir of excitement.

"Seventy-five thousand bucks—that's what I gave for that rock!" Phil Deming boasted, as he held up his wife's hand and displayed the huge diamond gleaming on one of her fingers. "Seventy-five thousand bucks—an' it's worth more'n that!"

Suddenly, Carlo Maggi was at his side, bending over the race-track operator, arguing with him. By coaxing and cajolery, he tried to quiet the man, turn his conversation into other, less attention-provoking channels. But Deming saw that he had the center of the limelight, and basked in it.

"Seventy-five thousand bucks!" he repeated more loudly than before and grinned with appreciation when every eye turned toward him. "Whatsa matter—can't I talk in here? Can't even talk to my friends, eh? Well—" he glanced at his watch—"it's nearly four o'clock. You gotta close up in a coupla minutes, but I know a place where they don't close—an'where I can talk. Down in the Village, to the Lost Gardens—that's where we're goin'."

His arising seemed to be a signal for a general exodus. Nearly half the patrons rose to their feet, and, despite Maggi's protests, a dozen or more started toward the door. In the confusion, Wentworth suddenly noticed that young Crosby was no longer at his table, and that Preston Kendall also had disappeared. Quickly, he reconnoitered the bar, the washroom. Just as he stepped into the corridor, he almost bumped into Kendall coming out of a phone booth. But of Allen Crosby there was no sign.

Had he gone along with Deming and his party? In the confusion that might have happened. But Wentworth wanted to stay very close to young Crosby that night.

Hailing a taxi, he gave the driver the Houston Street address of the all-night Village rendezvous—and saw the last of the Deming party going down the steps to the basement entrance, just as his cab turned into the block. Wentworth tried to follow, but, when he knocked on the door, a man behind the narrow slit of glass, that served as a lookout post, shook his head vigorously.

"Closed," he shouted gruffly. "After four o'clock. Can't let nobody in at this hour."

Wentworth knew that the Lost Gardens only started to do business at four o'clock. Yet now it was closed—after a party had just been admitted. Deming's foolish boasting, Kendall's coming out of that phone booth, the closed speakeasy—all these facts began to fall into place, to click with Stanley Kirkpatrick's theory….

Wentworth had to get into that establishment, but the

doorman had already turned away. Trying to force an entrance through the front would be useless. Quickly, he climbed back to the street level and regarded the outside of the building. The speakeasy occupied the basement. Above it was a store and six floors of tenements. Everything was dark except for a dim light in the hallway....

HIS RING of skeleton keys made short work of opening the old-fashioned lock on the door. Then he was padding up quietly through the stale-smelling hallway until he reached the top floor and climbed up to the roof. On the back of the house was a fire-escape, a rickety affair that squeaked and rasped under his weight. At every step, he expected to be challenged by awakened tenants, but reached the rubbish-cluttered yard without interference.

From the rear the Lost Gardens was as dark as from the front. But Wentworth located a grimy window that opened after his glass-cutter had gone to work on the pane. That window admitted him to a storeroom that opened onto a dark corridor. Cautiously, he stepped into the narrow hallway... and froze when he caught the sound of a woman's scream that cut short and choked back into her throat! That scream was drowned out by a flood of gruff, obscene curses!

Now there were more sounds from the front of the basement—sounds that chilled the blood in his veins as he crept closer to them.

To his left, he found the door of a small kitchen. There was nobody in it, and he stepped inside, cat-footed over to the little service window that looked out onto the main room—and found an unobstructed view of the nearest approach to hell he had ever seen!

In less than fifteen minutes the Lost Gardens had become a ghastly, blood-spattered shambles! Tied up and cowering on the floor at one side of the room were the proprietor, cook and two waiters—all staring glassy-eyed at where a dozen thugs worked horribly over the helpless prisoners who were lashed to chairs in the center of the room. Three couples had accompanied the Demings on that trip downtown—and of the eight merry-makers only the Demings still seemed to be alive!

Lashed helplessly to their chairs, the prisoners had been stripped of nearly all of their clothing—garments slashed from their bodies by keen-edged knives now dripping with blood. Knives that had been buried in their hearts as the blood-mad killers ruthlessly eliminated the witnesses who might have identified them!

Wentworth recoiled in utter horror from that ghastly slaughter. Savage, dope-crazed beasts let loose upon helpless captives! Barbarous torture and murder that made his blood boil with fierce rage!

"Where is it?" the burly leader of the thugs snarled again, as his knife blade sank into Phil Deming's shoulder and twisted cruelly. "Where's that rock? You had it when you came down here—now where is it?"

Deming's head lifted a scant two inches and then dropped back onto his bloody chest. But his wife moaned and shook her mouth free of the hand that clamped it shut.

"We haven't got it, I tell you!" she sobbed. "I took it off and dropped it on the floor when I saw what we were in for. One of your own crowd has it—oh, God, don't hurt him any more! Kill him, if you are going to, but don't hurt him any more! Oh, my God—*won't someone stop him?*"

Brutally, a hand clamped over her mouth and bent her head back so that she nearly choked. But in that moment her sobbing prayer was indeed answered.

Suddenly, that horribly quiet room echoed with a wild, maniacal laugh, a half-animal scream that chilled the blood and struck cold terror into the hearts of those mad killers. That scream came from the doorway that led to the kitchen—and there, beneath the plaster archway, crouched a twisted, stooped figure in a long black cape and black felt hat.

Out from beneath the floppy brim of that hat peered glistening eyes that gleamed from deep caverns in an incredibly hideous face—a sallow-skinned face, deeply lined and wrinkled, gashed by an ugly scar of a mouth and bloodless lips drawn back from snaggly teeth.

For an infinitesimal fraction of a second the grotesque specter crouched there—and then suddenly seemed to be all over the room, guns blasting death on every side.

"The Spider!" shrieked in wild panic from the lips of a killer, who pitched headlong as a bullet smashed through his face. Then that room of death became a roaring bedlam.

Knives streaked at that midnight-hued figure, guns blazed at him, terror-maddened men sprang at him with bare, clawing hands. But the Spider's deadly guns roared until they were empty; roared until he turned them into blood-dripping flails.

In the midst of the raging mêlée, the last light was shot out, and, a moment later, the opening of the front door clove a streak of dim light in the stygian darkness.

Shadowy figures scurried and dived for the doorway. Two of them gained it, a third… but the fourth went down with those black arms wound tightly around him, and stayed down when an automatic muzzle crashed through his skull. Over his body, the Spider scrambled… but now the quiet street was echoing with the shrill scream of sirens. Blue uniforms raced to the head of the stairs and blasted lead down into the basement.

Richard Wentworth waited for no more. Swiftly, he picked his way back through that ghastly shambles, and out through the rear door into the yard and over a fence. As he went, he stripped off the ugly make-up he had donned in such record time, ripped off the black cape and hat… and, when he came out through a cellar entrance into the street beyond, every evidence of the Spider was removed.

That foray had been almost in vain. The Spider had arrived too late to save the brutally massacred victims. But now the inhuman devils, who were behind this outrage, would know that the Spider was on their trail—and that Preston Kendall's best acting would not avail to save him from the doom decreed for him!

Here was the challenge….

CHAPTER 3
MURDER MISSION

W HEN RICHARD WENTWORTH awoke the next morning, Jenkyns, his butler, had already brought in the newspapers—papers which vied with one another in relating the gory details of the Village massacre. That brazen outrage had dwarfed everything else—even shoved into second place the gassing of the Standard Investment directors and Gilbert Crosby's suicide.

Of the eight who had left the Savoy Club for the Lost Gardens, only Evelyn Deming had still been alive when the police flashed their lights into the wrecked speakeasy. Only Evelyn Deming... and she had fainted before they arrived.

Her story of her own rescue was vague and incoherent, and the testimony of the owner and his employees proved little more helpful. A black-masked man had burst in from the rear and shot it out with the killers, they related—but they carefully refrained from any mention of the Spider. What they had seen was locked behind their lips for fear that the swift vengeance which had overtaken the killers would also be visited upon them.

"The Thanksgiving Eve Massacre" the newspapers had labeled the murders. Thanksgiving Day—it seemed queer that men should give thanks when such a ghastly atrocity could be committed in the heart of the greatest city in the world, Wentworth mused bitterly. The Pilgrim Fathers had been safer escorting their families to church, in the New England wilderness, than people were today in the midst of Manhattan....

It reminded Wentworth that he had promised to take Nita van Sloan to church that morning.

"We're going with the Claybornes, Dick," Nita greeted him when he arrived at her apartment. "Dorothy phoned last night to invite us, and a little while ago she called to be sure that we are coming. They attend St. Bartholomew's—and the Thanksgiving service there is supposed to be especially nice."

Rufus Clayborne was the president of a large importing house and an officer of fashionable St. Bartholomew's. Wentworth knew him and his family well and had often met Dorothy when she was calling on Nita. Joining their party was a pleasure, and by the time the service was finished Wentworth had almost forgotten the horror of the night before. He had almost forgotten, too, that the members of this exclusive congregation were all drawn from the high social stratum lately so prominent in the criminal news.

As the great organ pealed out the recessional, the parishioners filed out through the wide doors and down the steps onto Park Avenue. Nita and Wentworth were in the doorway before she realized that she had left her handkerchief in the pew.

"I know just where it is, Dick." She waved aside his offer to return for it. "It will take me only a moment—wait here for me."

Wentworth waited just past the threshold. He stood there chatting with the Claybornes and idly looking out over the smartly dressed throng spreading out over the avenue—when suddenly a wild alarm rang in his subconscious mind!

From the corner of his eye, he had glimpsed something that he instinctively knew was not as it should be. Something white across the way—a tablecloth or a sheet waving out of a window of the fashionable apartment house that stood opposite the church. In itself, that might not have registered on his brain, but at the same moment an ambulance came sirening down the avenue—a dusky-faced driver at the wheel.

That much Wentworth glimpsed, instantly. In the same moment, he flung himself backward in a frantic dive that caught Nita in the ribs and slapped her back into the people who were coming out from behind. She slammed against the side of the doorway just as the whole world seemed to disintegrate in a tremendous, deafening explosion.

Even as he went down, Wentworth's eyes missed no slightest detail of what was transpiring out there on the avenue. His camera-clear gaze spotted that brown-faced driver, another dark-skinned man inside the ambulance close against the driver's seat—finally focused on the ashen-faced man who suddenly bobbed up beside the man at the wheel and hurled something straight at the church door.

It was Larry Odell—Wentworth would have recognized this man anywhere!

Now the air seemed to be choked with the acrid tang of cordite, literally filled with flying debris-shattered stone and ghastly bits of what a moment before, had been human beings! Hushed silence crowded close on the heels of that ear-splitting detonation… then was torn by groans and shrieks of agony. Dazedly, Wentworth got to his feet and bent anxiously over Nita. The side of her coat was torn and blood was soaking her left sleeve—but, thank God, her eyes were open and unafraid. She was getting to her knees, looking around, and stark horror flared in her eyes.

"I'm all right," she gasped as she got to her feet. "But the others… Dorothy…."

MORE THAN a score of people lay scattered like broken, discarded dolls on the wreckage-littered sidewalk—people who were ripped and torn fearfully, many of them mangled so that they were hardly recognizable. And among them, at one side of the shattered steps, lay Rufus Clayborne and his daughter.

Dorothy was on her knees, crawling slowly to where her father lay supine. Before she could reach him, Wentworth was at his side, lifting the old man's blood-soaked head. One glance at Clayborne's frightful wounds told him that the old gentleman could not possibly survive, if life had not already flown from his battered body.

But the gray eyes opened, the torn lips moved feebly. "I would not do what they told me," Clayborne whispered wetly. "I would not be a thief—no matter what they threatened. I knew… they would… get me… but I didn't… expect this…."

"Daddy! Daddy!" Dorothy Clayborne moaned. "Why didn't you tell me? I didn't know. I didn't know that they threatened you, too. They told me they would ruin and kill you unless I brought Nita and Dick here with us today. They said that was all

I would have to do—just bring them here. I didn't know, Daddy. I thought surely we would all be safe here in the crowd—*I didn't know!*"

But Rufus Clayborne did not hear her. The faded gray eyes stared sightlessly up at the blue November sky. Nita drew the girl away from him, held her limp body until Wentworth lifted her and carried her into the church which was being converted into an improvised hospital and morgue.

A dozen times, as he labored doing his best to ease the suffering of the other victims, Wentworth returned to look down at her still face—but Dorothy Clayborne did not reopen her eyes.

"It's a wonder she lived as long as she did." The ambulance surgeon, who examined her, shook his head in surprise. "Her whole chest is crushed in—battered to a pulp."

Dorothy Clayborne was dead—and once more Death had diabolically stepped in to seal the lips which might have furnished a clue to the inhuman devils behind this monstrous horror. Grim-eyed, stern-jawed, Wentworth looked down at those rows of sufferers and those others who were now beyond suffering. Nearly twenty people wantonly murdered… why?

To punish him for interfering or attempting to interfere with the deviltry that was decimating the ranks of his friends? To punish Rufus Clayborne for refusing the demands of this robbery and murder ring? Probably for both of those reasons—a cunningly devised double-edged stroke, Wentworth decided. Once more the wily criminals had left no trace behind them, no clue to follow.

The ambulance had disappeared, a way through traffic opened

for it by the unsuspecting police…The window from which that white signal had been flown proved to be in an empty apartment.

Not a clue, except Larry Odell….

AS SOON as he was able to take Nita back to her apartment, Wentworth started on Odell's trail. At his home, at his club, his known rendezvous—one after the other Wentworth searched. His man was at none of them, had not been seen all day. But Wentworth did pick up one significant bit of information: Odell had been attentive to Mildred Taylor, old Hamilton Taylor's missing daughter.

By ten o'clock that night Wentworth gave up the quest and went back to Sutton Place. Entering by way of the dummy apartment that fronted on the street, he went through the underground passage to his stronghold in the rear. The moment he stepped out of the elevator in the rear building, Jackson was there to meet him. The chauffeur's face was grave, his eyes worried. "I have been trying to locate you for the past two hours, sir," Jackson said quickly. "A few minutes before that we received a telephone call that you were badly hurt and that an ambulance was bringing you home. I opened the gates when it arrived. Before I could close them again, two dark-skinned men—Hindus they appeared to be—jumped out and covered me with their guns. They ran out of the drive and were picked up by a car on the corner."

He went on. "When I got a close look at the ambulance I almost tumbled off the running-board. There was a dead man on the seat, and a dead woman in the back—a woman that devils had been working on!"

"Where is that ambulance now?"

"I knew you wouldn't want it out there in the drive—in case we should happen to have visitors," Jackson told him. "I ran it into one of the garages and then lowered it underground."

He led the way to a row of garages on the side street at one end of Wentworth's property, pressed a button on the wall when they were inside. Slowly most of the cement floor began to disappear, slid in under one of the walls. Up from below rose a new floor—a floor on which the death ambulance stood, with its corpse passenger still propped up on the seat beside the wheel.

Wentworth took one glance at that staring eyed corpse and recognized Larry Odell. Then he was at the rear of the car, opening the door and stepping inside, to stare down in nauseous horror at the atrociously mutilated body of Mildred Taylor!

Now he knew why Larry Odell had become a desperate killer. He must have seen what the devils were doing to his sweetheart. In order to halt their hellish work, he had dealt sudden death to a score of unsuspecting church people on the steps of their house of worship! Only the mind of a fiend from the Pit itself could have conceived such a frightful weapon to hold over a man's head—and such an appalling way to use it....

For more than two hours that corpse-laden ambulance had been there—and yet the police had not come seeking it. That meant that this was no frame-up but a sardonic warning. It meant that the fiend who had decreed the St. Bartholomew's slaughter knew that Wentworth had escaped—and had sent this taunting warning to greet him the very moment he returned!

But who could that master murderer be? Someone who had

been in the Savoy Club last night when Phil Deming had made his foolish boast: someone who had quickly set the stage for the Village holdup the moment Deming had announced his destination. Preston Kendall seemed the most likely suspect— Preston Kendall coming out of the phone booth after calling his Underworld allies. But Kendall could not be alone in this. He did not have the acquaintance or social entree to have engineered all these other baffling crimes which had the police at a standstill. He might be one of the gang, but there were others.

One by one, Wentworth recalled the other guests who had been near Phil Deming when he rose to leave the Savoy. One by one—until he came to Gooja Singh, the Hindu! Two dark-skinned men—two Hindus—had brought that death-laden ambulance to Wentworth's door. They might have been two of Gooja Singh's men—or Gooja Singh, himself, with one of his fellows!

Wentworth knew the man slightly, had a nodding acquaintance with him, but now he determined to press that acquaintance farther. There were several questions he wanted to ask Gooja Singh—questions which it would not require a mystic's power to answer.

ONE AFTER the other, Wentworth toured the night-clubs where the Hindu was generally to be found. Gooja Singh was in none of them, but any number of people were able to supply his address—a four-story brownstone on a side street off Central Park West. Wentworth approached the building in a taxicab, stopped in front of the house next door and started to alight—

only to draw back from the door and peer out at a man coming down the steps of the Hindu's residence.

Milo Spencer, the mystic-prosecutor, keeping a midnight rendezvous with Gooja Singh!

Wentworth stared at the man in surprise. He caught a glimpse of his thin, acetic face as the rays of an arc-light played on it momentarily. Spencer was smiling to himself. His lips were moving soundlessly, repeating the conversation he must have finished, and his features were a curious mask of crafty satisfaction.

After the crusader had passed and walked to the corner, Wentworth paid off his driver and mounted the stone steps. A light was burning in Gooja Singh's hallway, and an Oriental-clad doorman promptly answered the bell. Politely, he ushered Wentworth into an anteroom and then escorted him into an inner room that was completely hung with Oriental rugs and draperies. It was dimly lit with almost opaque lanterns hanging from wall brackets and by one overhead globe that played full upon a small center table and the chair behind it.

In the center of that table stood a great crystal ball, so large that it extended beyond the edges. In the chair behind it sat Gooja Singh, resplendent in jewel-studded turban and rich East Indian robes.

"Good evening, Mr. Wentworth," he greeted as he rose and extended his hand—and Wentworth had the peculiar feeling that the man had been expecting him, even waiting there for him to arrive. "You have come to consult me—because you are in difficulties." The Hindu nodded slowly as he waved his hand toward a seat on the opposite side of the crystal. "Because there are questions you want answered—"

"You seem to know," Wentworth acknowledged.

"Not I," the Hindu deprecated. "Such knowledge as I may have is due to my extra-sensory perception, to my inherited ability to establish contact with the truth which is hidden from most men."

"Perhaps, then," Wentworth's poker face was inscrutable, "you will be able to identify for me two men of your race who drive an ambulance in this city."

Keenly, he watched Gooja Singh's lean, brown face. But the dark eyes gave no sign of surprise. Not a muscle in that inscrutable countenance betrayed the slightest indication that the question was in any way pointed.

"Perhaps I shall," Gooja Singh agreed. "If you will please cooperate with me by concentrating on the crystal."

He must have touched a button, for the overhead light snapped off and, at the same instant, the crystal began to glow feebly. Slowly, the light became stronger, until the whole sphere shone and cast a milky illumination on their faces.

"Yes—" Gooja Singh's voice was hardly more than a whisper—"I see that you are in difficulties—difficulties which you have brought upon yourself. Yes, I see men of my own race surrounding you, and others, also—men with guns and with keen-bladed, deadly weapons. Behind them I see another figure—a dominating figure but one whose features I cannot distinguish. He is a man of power and implacable determination—one it is extremely unwise to cross."

42

For a moment, the low voice was still. Then it resumed, a silky voice now edged with unmistakable threat.

"I see you in great trouble, Mr. Wentworth," Gooja Singh said slowly. "I see your body lying on the street. I see those who love you weeping over your bier. I see the dominant figure striding onward after you are no longer in his path. I see that you may still avoid this fate if you are wise. There is a proverb in the East: 'A wise man needs no warning; only a fool will ignore it.'"

Wentworth's hand was at his coat pocket, slipped into it and closed on the butt of the automatic he had cached ready there—but at that moment the crystal ball seemed to become alive with figures. Dark faces peered out at him: dark figures hovered with keen-bladed knives poised for a deadly plunge, for a fatal flip. Reflections craftily revealed in the gleaming sphere—wordlessly, they told him that he was surrounded, that his life would be forfeit at the first hostile move.

"Yes," Gooja Singh's voice became faintly mocking, "there is trouble for you in the crystal, Mr. Wentworth—deadly trouble that surrounds you inescapably on every side and against which your weapons will be useless. Trouble such as there was for Stuart Johnson, who involved you in his difficulties and then was so foolish as to talk to the police. In the crystal it is revealed to me that Mr. Johnson has made atonement for his error, but that you still have an opportunity—"

Every nerve tense, Wentworth listened, watched—then he saw his opportunity!

Gooja Singh had moved back slightly—sufficiently so that Wentworth would be able to fling himself to one side, around that crystal ball, and jab the automatic into the Hindu's ribs. The balls of his feet pressed into the thick carpet, the palm of his left hand hardened against the arm of the chair—but the moment he started to rise the chair gave way beneath him, the very floor fell away from under his feet!

Desperately, he triggered his automatic. The crystal ball shattered into a thousand pieces, bullets ripped harmlessly into the walls and ceiling… but he was going down, down into blackness that suffocated him, that clutched at his throat and shut off his breath. Frantically, he tried to fight his way up through what seemed to be great masses of smothering featherbeds, but they engulfed him, buried him deeper and deeper, until even the sound of Gooja Singh's mocking laughter dwindled and then faded out miles and miles away....

WENTWORTH'S HANDS felt thick and bloated when he closed them on the arms of his chair. His head was like a great balloon, his eyes leaden-lidded. For long minutes he sat there before he could force himself to open his eyes and stare around him in the darkness.

Gradually, he became accustomed to the faint light from a window. Now he saw that he was in an office, sitting in a chair beside a desk. He got to his feet, groped his way to a wall and located the light switch. Next moment he was staring across a wide, flat-topped desk to where the dead body of Stuart Johnson slumped in his chair!

Stuart Johnson, with a bullet hole through his temple!

On the floor beside the chair lay an automatic—one of Wentworth's own. He picked it up, sniffed it. The barrel was rank with the taint of a recently fired shot. One of the cartridges in the clip was discharged—and that bullet, he knew, was in Stuart Johnson's brain.

Those thoughts had hardly penetrated his still numbed mind when he heard footsteps outside in the hall, the sound of a key in the lock. Against the glass door panel, he caught the silhouette of a police-capped head. Then he snapped back to normal, darting into the next room as he frenziedly now sought a way of hurried escape.

The windows of that next office opened on a narrow ledge that ran across the front of the building. It was a chance—the only one.

Quickly Wentworth got one of the windows open, climbed out onto the narrow ledge and closed the window behind him. Dizzily, not daring to look down at the fifteen-story drop beside him, he edged his way along from window to window, teetering sickeningly on the brink of eternity.

He passed six windows before he dared to give the pane a swift crack with his automatic. Then he reached inside, turned the catch.

Nobody was in the hall when he cautiously opened the office door; nor did anybody stop him, as he darted across the twenty-foot space to the stairway door and trudged slowly down to the street level.

A perfect murder set-up, he admitted grimly. Gooja Singh had tried him out with a warning, but when that was ignored the wily Hindu had been ready with an effective way to eliminate him. They could easily have killed him, Wentworth realized.

But this punishment evidently appealed more strongly to the Hindu's Oriental mind. It also would serve as a public example to anyone else who might be tempted to horn in or interfere.

Except for Wentworth's last-minute escape, round one had been entirely Gooja Singh's. Cunningly he had seen to it that there was not the slightest chance to prove a thing against him....

CHAPTER 4
TERROR TRAIL

STUART JOHNSON'S murder would have been sensational news at any other time, but the morning papers relegated it to an inside page as they featured the Park Avenue bombing and the discovery of the murder ambulance with its corpse cargo. The ambulance had been located in the early hours of the morning, standing beside the curb on a side street near the East River.

A dozen wild theories for the double tragedy were advanced, with most of the writers suspecting that young Odell had gone berserk because the Taylor girl had rejected his suit. However, Commissioner Kirkpatrick took the discovery as added confirmation of his own suspicions.

"A thing like this could not have been accomplished without inside cooperation," he repeated when Wentworth went to the morgue to help identify the body of the bomb-thrower. "New York society is being victimized from within—by some playboy who is putting his finger on his friends and turning them over to the Underworld. Someone who is well acquainted with society's intimate affairs—with its romances, its scandals and its careless little habits that lay it open to attack."

He nodded. "This fellow, whoever he is, was present in the Savoy Club when Phil Deming made an ass of himself—he tipped off the gangsters who slaughtered the Deming party. The night-clubs are his hunting ground, and I'll locate him there if I have to close up every club in town. John Petrillo is bringing most of the owners to my office this afternoon. I know how you feel about Gilbert Crosby and the Taylors, Dick. If you want to, come down and sit in on that session."

But Wentworth had other plans for that day. Kirkpatrick might be on the right track, but the murderous criminal who was behind this reign of terror, would not be trapped by conferences of harried and bulldozed night-club owners.

Despite the denials of Anice Crosby and her mother, Wentworth was convinced that they were in constant danger—that it was to discourage his own attempts in their behalf that Gooja Singh had first warned and then tried to frame him. For that reason, he assigned Jackson to the task of keeping a constant watch on the Crosby residence.

"I want to know of everyone who goes and comes from that house," he instructed, "and I want you to be ready to get help at a moment's notice if there is any attempt made on the girl or her mother."

Leaving Jackson to cover that angle, he went uptown to the lavish penthouse apartment that had been Phil Deming's. Evelyn Deming, an attractive young woman with auburn hair

and blue eyes, invited him in as
soon as she heard that his call
was in regard to the death of
her husband.

Wentworth studied her
carefully, as he questioned her
about the night of the tragedy,
and as he watched his satisfaction increased. The young widow
was grief-stricken, but not prostrated—beneath her anguish
smoldered a fierce thirst for revenge.

"At least three or four of those beasts escaped," she said
bitterly, "and I only hope that I meet them again sometime. I
would know them anywhere, I am sure. Even though they were
masked, I stared at each of them so steadily during those awful
minutes that I memorized every feature, every mannerism of
theirs. All that I ask now is that I have a chance to identify them
to square the account for Phil and the others."

"That is why I came to see you," Wentworth told her. Carefully he outlined the plan which he hoped would lead him to
the man who was responsible for those murders and a score of
other tragedies as well.

Evelyn Deming held out her hand, and her grip was firm, her
blue eyes level and unflinching as she gave her word.

The rest of that day Wentworth searched in vain for Preston
Kendall. A brief notice in the theatrical section of the papers
had announced his temporary withdrawal from the cast of *The
Green Goddess* to nurse a cold, but he was not at his hotel and the
hotel people had no idea where he had gone. Finally, Wentworth

managed to corner the manager of the Continental Theater and force from him an admission that he likewise was in the dark as to the actor's whereabouts. He had received only a brief note from Kendall announcing that he was leaving town for a few days.

"When you've dealt with actors as long as I have, nothing they do surprises you," he shrugged resignedly. "They're all alike—but I thought Kendall wasn't quite as goofy as most of them."

Preston Kendall had disappeared, Gooja Singh was well fortified and no doubt prepared for another visit—but there still remained Milo Spencer. Spencer, who had been present in the Savoy Club when Phil Deming and his party were there; who had been coming out of Gooja Singh's establishment just before Wentworth arrived.

Wentworth had made guarded inquiries about the reformer, and the more he learned the more he began to suspect that Spencer's activities were quite different than was generally supposed. The office of his crusading organization was in his home—an office that should afford interesting revelations for an investigator....

IT WAS after the dinner hour before Wentworth made a blind telephone call to ascertain that Spencer was at home. From the opposite side of the street he studied the narrow, four-story building just off Stuyvesant Square and considered ways of entering it unobserved. The first floor had only a doorway and two windows in front, but in the rear....

At that moment the door opened and Spencer came out, walked to the corner and hailed a cab. Again Wentworth went to a phone booth and dialed the number, and this time there was no response. That meant there were no servants—the house was empty.

Boldly he approached the door, fitting a skeleton key to the lock. Once inside, he reconnoitered quickly and quietly, found that he had the place to himself. At the rear of the first floor, he located Spencer's office and went to work at the old man's desk. Milo Spencer was a careful man. There were plenty of papers, plenty of memoranda, in the orderly arranged drawers, but nothing in any way significant.

A pigeon-hole of his old-fashioned desk yielded a list of twenty Hindu names—with Gooja Singh's at the top. But beyond that there was nothing to indicate that his activities were not just what they were supposed to be. Turning from the desk, Wentworth located a wall safe behind a dummy panel—a simple combination that soon responded to his trained, sensitive fingers. But again the results were disappointing.

Milo Spencer's records were sparse and cabalistic—all except his bankbooks, which recorded deposits of thousands of dollars during the past two months. Those deposits were out of all proportion to his possible income. Wentworth also noticed that they had become much heavier since the crime wave had started to engulf New York's men of wealth and social position.

Could this wily old hypocrite, sitting secure in his self-appointed position of public protector, be the arch-villain who was preying on the city?

Only Milo Spencer, it seemed, could answer that question—if he would talk. Certainly, he would not talk to Richard

Wentworth. But there was an effective way of loosening recalcitrant lips....

Swiftly, Wentworth went to work with his make-up kit, and under the play of his skilled fingers his features changed form. Sallow, deep-lined skin replaced his healthy complexion; drops in his eyes made them glitter eerily. False teeth that were ugly and repulsive, bushy black eyebrows, a wig of stringy and matted black hair—each contributed its part to that transformation. When the black cloak and hat were in place, the Spider was waiting for Milo Spencer to return.

Carefully, he rearranged the books and papers in the safe and started to close it when his alert ears caught a sound at the front door. It was opening, closing again. Wentworth snapped off the light and leaned back against the desk, waiting. But there was no further sound—no footsteps after the door closed.

Had Spencer caught a glimpse of that light before it had been extinguished? Had he taken flight, managed to slip back out of the door?

Softly, Wentworth stepped into the hallway—just as the light snapped on and he found himself facing a masked man who covered him with a leveled revolver. Wentworth could easily have shot that gun out of the fellow's hand and killed him before he had time to press the trigger. But something about the man's tensity made him hold his fire.

"Back there where you came from!" the masked arrival ordered.

Wentworth backed, and a moment later the office lights again flashed on as his captor stood beside the switch, gun held ready.

"So," he breathed softly, "you are the Spider. I have heard of the Spider. Foe of criminals, noble defender of the oppressed, the man who rights the wrongs the incompetent police cannot handle—and you are Milo Spencer, a cheap, grafting blood-sucker who grows fat on the crooks and charlatans you are supposed to prosecute!"

His words dripped with contempt, with loathing.

"That doesn't interest me, Spencer—your racket was your own affair, until you started to work on me. But when you think you can make a cheap crook out of me, you have another guess coming. You think you are pretty slick—that nobody knows you are hand in glove with this crooked bunch of clairvoyants you pretend to expose. But I've had detectives on your trail, and I have you dead to rights."

He went on. "That's why I tried to decoy you out of here by that phone call half an hour ago. I gave you plenty of time to get out so that I could break in and wait for you to return—but it seems you were too cagey to fall for that standup date. That doesn't matter. I'm here now, and you are here—that's all I want now."

The revolver muzzle rose an inch higher—and the toe of Wentworth's foot hooked behind a leg of the chair beside him.

"Before you pull that trigger," he rasped in the discordant voice of the Spider, "there is something in this office you had better see."

He nodded toward the open door of the safe—and the masked man's eyes flickered in that direction for a fraction of a second. Barely a flash—it was all Wentworth needed. Flinging himself to one side, his foot overturned the solid wooden chair, tumbled it against the fellow's shins before he could leap clear. Twice his revolver roared, but the bullets bored into the wall, and then the gun fell from his fingers as one of Wentworth's automatics came down over his skull.

The moment the fellow had slumped to the floor the Spider was over him, kneeling beside him and tearing away the mask—to stare down into the face of Thad Darrington, one of the directors of the bank where he kept his own account!

Thad Darrington! Wentworth grasped him by the shoulders and shook him, but the banker was unconscious. At that moment there was a new commotion out at the door. Milo Spencer was returning—and with him he was bringing the police! The wily old fox had scented a trap when he discovered that Darrington's phone call was a fake. He had come back prepared for trouble.

Wentworth lifted the banker, tried to carry him; but Darrington weighed every bit of two hundred and fifty pounds. There was no choice but to leave him, his life at least safe now that the police were on hand....

Swiftly, Wentworth raised a window and dropped out into the back yard, ran its length and clambered over one fence after another, until he reached an alleyway that ran behind the corner building. In the darkness his fingers wiped away his Spider make-up, removed every vestige of it so that he could step out onto the street without fear of attracting attention.

So Thaddeus Darrington was the latest victim of the crime wave. But Darrington had rebelled and convinced himself that the man who was hounding him was Milo Spencer. Spencer, with the recently swollen bank account; Spencer, who was on visiting terms with the mystics upon whom he supposedly warred; Spencer, who had seen Evelyn Deming's ring held high in the Savoy Club....

THOSE THOUGHTS were still in Wentworth's mind the next afternoon when he drove to the cemetery to await Gilbert Crosby's funeral cortege. Jackson had reported nothing of importance from his vigil outside the Crosby home, but, with the terrible death of Mildred Taylor fresh in mind, Wentworth was taking no chances that a similar fate might overtake Anice Crosby.

When the coaches arrived at the family plot, he was waiting a short distance away in a screened vantage point from which he could keep watch on the proceedings. Behind the casket came Elizabeth Crosby with her son Allen, the elder Crosby daughter Margaret and her husband, Paul Nugent, Anice Crosby with....

Wentworth stared. Anice Crosby was with the young fellow who had leaped upon him the other night as he left the Crosby home! The fellow who had battled with him and escaped when Preston Kendall came to his rescue!

There was nothing otherwise unusual about that funeral;

nobody else there to furnish the slightest clue to the reason for Gilbert Crosby's amazing thievery and suicide. Wentworth's trip to the cemetery would have been wasted but for Anice's escort—but that discovery made it decidedly worth while.

After the interment, the funeral party disbanded. Only Mrs. Crosby, Allen, Anice and her escort returned to the Crosby home. Wentworth trailed them in a taxicab. From the street corner, he watched them enter the building and then started toward the door, prepared to announce himself and confront his assailant. But as he reached the house a sound from within set his nerves atingle.

It was a woman's scream, cut short in mid-cry! Then he heard the unmistakable sounds of a scuffle—and for an instant Allen Crosby was thrown back against the front door. Wentworth caught just a glimpse of Crosby's head and shoulders, his up-flung arm, before he was jerked out of sight—but that was sufficient.

Automatic in hand, Wentworth sprang into the vestibule and charged the inner door. Shattering the long glass pane, he leaped through the frame, flung himself into the hall—just as a knife whizzed past his ear and sank, quivering, into the oak-paneled wall.

In one all inclusive glance, he took in the situation. Mrs. Crosby and Anice were cowering against the wall at one side of the foyer, a dark-skinned fellow with a wicked-looking knife standing threateningly over them. Allen Crosby was on the floor, a Hindu astride him. Anice's escort was being hauled to his feet by another of the Orientals, while a fourth masked figure stood back and supervised operations. Unsuspectingly, the Crosbys had come home and stepped into a trap that awaited them just inside their door.

Already, the fellow who stood guard over the women had lashed Anice's hands in front of her, was jamming a gag into her mouth—but at that moment Wentworth's gun barrel hit him and set him spinning across the hall. In an instant, the others left their men, swarming about Wentworth, grasping his gun and wresting it from his fingers. Brown arms snaked out around his neck, a knife flashed within inches of his throat—but he wriggled out of that muscular embrace and sent his fist smashing into the face of the knife-wielder.

Savagely, Wentworth tore into those brown-skinned devils, pulping their faces with his fists, flinging them breathless and snarling across the foyer as he plucked the knives from their fingers and broke their arms with cruel *jiu-jitsu* grips. A whirlwind, mercilessly effective onslaught—it took the attackers by surprise, had them beaten back, almost at his mercy. Then, suddenly he was grabbed from behind—set upon by young Crosby and his companion!

Wentworth staggered back under that treacherous assault. He went to his knees, then was back on his feet, whirling to meet these new assailants. Grimly, he lashed out at them, pounded them with every ounce of his strength. Young Crosby doubled up and dropped, groaning, to the floor. Anice's escort tried desperately to protect his blood-spurting nose—then caromed crazily across the hall and into the adjoining room as Wentworth's fist caught him on the side of the jaw. They had had enough—but by that time the Hindus had seized the chance to escape. Through the shattered window of the door they had darted, and when Wentworth ran into the street there was no sign of them.

"NOW, WHAT'S it all about?" he demanded grimly when he strode back inside and hauled the bloody-faced youngster to his feet. "Working with those brown-skinned devils, were you? Trying to help them kidnap Anice!"

"No—no!" the fellow panted, mopping his face with a red-stained handkerchief. "I was trying to help her. I didn't understand. After I saw you outside the other night, I thought you were the one who was making all this trouble for her and her family. I heard you in here questioning them that night, believed you were trying to trick them. Then just now, when you came again, I was sure of it!"

"Who are you?" Wentworth snapped.

"Wesley Brewster," the youngster identified himself as the son of a well known socialite family. "Anice is going to be my fiancée."

"And you—" Wentworth swung on young Crosby—"why were you so ready to pile into me?"

"We've had so much trouble," Allen Crosby floundered uncertainly. "I didn't know—I thought you were with them. During the past few weeks, I have had no peace. I've been threatened—warned that I would be killed. It's gotten so that I distrust and suspect everybody. I didn't know—"

Young Crosby wasn't a good liar. Wentworth could see that he was desperately afraid of something—that he would not reveal what he was holding back no matter how hard pressed. Both Crosby and Brewster undoubtedly were lying. Only Anice and her mother, completely bewildered by everything that was happening, seemed genuine. The girl was sobbing in the old lady's arms, but now raised her tear-stained face and eyed him frankly.

"I didn't tell you the truth when you questioned me the other day, Mr. Wentworth," she admitted. "I *have* been afraid—terribly afraid. There have been men following me. I have seen them slinking around the house—have felt their eyes on me constantly. I have been in terror of being kidnaped, afraid that they would—"

Suddenly her lips clamped shut, and she turned away.

"Afraid that they would *what?*" Wentworth pressed.

But now her confession was silenced by a warning look from one of the others. "Oh, I don't know!" she sobbed hysterically, when he persisted. "That's all—anything else is just my imagination!"

With that Wentworth had to be content. Crosby and Brewster were evasive, and, now that her terror was mastered, Anice was as noncommittal as they. The lips of all three, he suspected, were sealed by the same threat that had driven Gilbert Crosby to self-destruction—a stone wall of silence against which it was useless to butt his head.

Nonplussed, he started to leave, then stooped to pick up something that gleamed on the floor. A large, oval-shaped opal—a gem that he had seen before. Where? He wracked his memory, then had it! That gem, or its twin, had been set in a ring on the finger of Gooja Singh! And it had been dropped here by one of those masked Hindu attackers....

It was after eleven o'clock that night when Wentworth's telephone rang, and a tense voice came to him over the wire.

"I have found them—two of them!" Evelyn Deming spoke softly into the mouthpiece. "They are here in the Armageddon Club. They knew who I am—know that I've recognized them. I am trapped in the ladies' room… and I know they will kill me if I try to leave!"

Before he could answer, the connection was broken.

CHAPTER 5
BATTLE WITH BEASTS

PHIL DEMING would not have known his widow could he have seen her as she stepped into the Armageddon Club. Her auburn hair had been bleached to platinum blonde and her face was made up as it never had been during his lifetime. A flashy, inviting-looking charmer, for two nights she had been going from one night-club to another, her long-lashed, heavily mascarraed eyes watchfully scanning the bar, flitting from table to table. But it was not until she stepped into the bar of the Armageddon that she found what she was seeking.

There, at the farther end of the polished mahogany rail, was a face she would have recognized anywhere. A handsome, dark-eyed face—she had glimpsed it only once before, but that had ingrained it on her memory. Only once—when Phil Deming had momentarily knocked askew the mask that covered it. That

THE DEVIL'S CANDLESTICKS

Bullets were flying everywhere—smashing into walls and mirrors, cutting down terrified guests!

smirking dandy was one of the bestial killers who had staged the Lost Gardens massacre!

There was an empty bar-stool beside the fellow, and a moment later Evelyn Deming was seated on it, exchanging glances with him in the back-bar mirror. When her drink accidentally overturned, and splashed the arm of his coat, they became acquainted.

"That's nothing at all." He grinned when she tried to apologize. "Forget about it. But—"his dark eyes glowed at her—"you're not comfortable here. That's why you spilled your drink. Suppose we go inside and have a table? You and me and—Jim here?"

That was all right with her, although it did not seem to be particularly pleasing to heavy-jowled Jim. He glowered and grunted something but came along, to sit back in his chair and regard his sheikish companion with obvious disapproval.

"His name is Jim," Evelyn Deming probed when the waiter had taken their order, "and yours is—"

"Tony." The dandy smirked. "Tony Marino. That big sourmug is Jim Belotti—and you, I guess you're just Blondie."

"Mary—Mary O'Neill," she told him and led him on to talk about himself. But all the while she was aware of Jim Belotti's sharp scrutiny.

Even when his drink arrived, his heavy-lidded eyes did not leave her face. Absent-mindedly he reached for his glass—and the blood pounded faster in her veins as she glimpsed the forefinger of his right hand. At some time it had been smashed, and the nail had never grown back properly. The scarred nail was unmistakable. The last time she had seen that nail Jim Belotti's blunt fingers had been curled around a knife that was digging cruelly into Phil Deming's shoulder!

Her eyes must have widened with surprise, betrayed her before she could control them. Now Belotti was fairly glaring at her. He had caught her looking at that nail—and understood what her agitation meant!

"Seems to me I seen you somewhere before." He leaned forward on the table, and frowned. "You sure your name is Mary O'Neill?"

Evelyn Deming managed to laugh her way out of that. But she saw that the man was not convinced. Now she caught the sudden glint of satisfaction in his murky eyes that told he had recognized her! Now there wasn't a moment to lose. Excusing herself, she started to the ladies' room—but Belotti was close at her side to see that she went nowhere else.

Fortunately, there was a telephone in the washroom. An open phone, but she managed to call Richard Wentworth's number and deliver her message before two other women came in.

From the doorway, she could see the table she had just left. Belotti was leaning over it, talking excitedly to his companion. Marino's smiling face had become bleak, deadly. Belotti signaled to the bar, and another man joined them, listened for a moment and then left. Now Belotti's eyes were again glued to the ladies' room door. She could not possibly leave without being seen.

For nearly fifteen minutes, Evelyn Deming cowered there, counting each second and trying desperately to find a way of escape. Then there was a new arrival at the killers' table—a tall, hard-looking girl who listened to Belotti's instructions, nodded, and walked across the room.

She was out of sight for a few moments. Then she stood right there in the washroom doorway; a deadly-looking little revolver, gripped in her hand, was jammed against Evelyn Deming's ribs.

"Outside," she ordered softly. "You've kept the boys waiting too long. They want to take you places."

Helplessly, like a doomed convict being led to the execution chamber, Evelyn Deming stepped out into the main room....

JACKSON HAD one of Wentworth's cars at the door in record time; was speeding out through the gates the moment Wentworth sprang on the running-board and dropped into the seat beside him. Straight across town to the Armageddon Club they drove, while Wentworth gave swift directions.

"We're barely in time," he noted, as they glided into an open space at the curb just as a girl and four men got out of a taxi and went into the club. The men first glanced up and down the street searchingly and then stepped forward like jungle cats—killers all set.

"I'll go in through the main doorway—you come in and cover me from the bar," Wentworth outlined when they were in the reception hall. Then he strode into the modernistically decorated dining-room that was John Petrillo's pride. He stepped through the doorway barely in time to see Evelyn Deming, white-faced and tense, make her slow entrance from the ladies' room.

Like an automaton, she walked half a dozen steps, her eyes staring, fascinated, at the table where two men were rising, moving forward to intercept her. Half a dozen steps—and then she broke. Leaping away from the girl who was close at her side, she tried to dart into the hall. The sleek-haired, devilishly smiling member of that pair intercepted her. His hand darted out, whirled her around, pulled her close against him.

Fearfully, she stared up into his cruelly gloating face, and then a scream broke from her lips as she struggled desperately to break away. Deliberately, he twisted her arm up behind her back, bent her forward and forced her toward the door... where Wentworth stepped out to meet them.

For an instant their eyes clashed—then the fellow's free hand streaked for his gun. Before he could reach it, Wentworth's fist pounded into his face and smashed that mocking smirk from his lips. Stepping in upon him quickly, Wentworth grasped the girl and thrust her behind him as he whirled to meet the attack that he knew would come from all parts of the room.

Those four killers who had arrived in the taxi had spread out fan-wise so as to dominate every corner of the place. Now their hands were reaching for their guns. The heavy-jowled, snarling individual, who had arisen with the sheik, already had an automatic in his hand. It thundered—and Wentworth felt the hot breath of a bullet that whistled past his ear. The searing furrow of a second slug grooved in his shoulder.

Like a charging bull, that big fellow came blundering heedlessly through the panic-stricken guests—until a black hole mushroomed magically in the center of his forehead, and he pitched headlong on his face.

Seizing one of the nearest tables, Wentworth up-ended it and shoved it in front of Evelyn Deming, where she crouched trembling against the wall. Then he whirled to meet the murderous-eyed dandy just as the fellow got to his feet. Smashing his gun out of his hand, Wentworth pistol-whipped him across the face and sent him staggering backward—into the path of a bullet that wrung a scream of agony from his bloodied lips.

But now guns seemed to be roaring from every side of the big room. Bullets were flying everywhere, smashing into walls and mirrors, cutting down the terrified guests frantically scrambling out of the way. Crouched close above Evelyn Deming, Wentworth tried to protect her with his own body. But bullets were splintering the table, and her screams were keening in his ears as he triggered lead at the killers.

Two of them he blasted out of action—but there seemed to be half a dozen more. They were converging on him from two sides. That meant it would be only a matter of seconds before he was flanked and cut down, before they would swarm over him.

Grabbing another table, he propped it up in front of Evelyn Deming and turned to risk everything in a desperate charge. And at that moment Jackson came blasting his way across the wrecked dining room, with John Petrillo at his side and half a dozen waiters at his back. Blazing-eyed, Petrillo shot down those killers, mercilessly—seized them and battered them with his bare hands when his gun was empty.

That reinforcement routed the gangsters. Wildly, they scrambled for safety, leaving their wounded fellows where they had fallen; and in another minute the Armageddon was cleared.

"Those are the ones!" Evelyn Deming gasped as Wentworth

helped her to her feet. "That big one—his name is Jim Belotti. This one who had hold of me—he is Tony Marino."

"Maybe that's what they told you, Miss." John Petrillo was shaking his head as he looked down at the killers she indicated. "The big fellow is Oreste Galento—and this other one, he is Salvatore Tresca. They are men I don't like in my place—but what can one do?"

GALENTO WAS quite dead, but Tresca was still breathing, Wentworth noticed; and immediately he was at the fellow's side, was raising his head and offering him a drink. Tresca's eyes opened and gleamed evilly when he realized what had happened. Softly curses whispered from his lips.

"I don't blame you, Tresca," Wentworth sympathized. "It's a pretty rotten feeling to know that you've been double-crossed. But a wise bird like you should have known better than to trust any of these society kids. You might have known what would happen."

Tresca's eyes became seething pools of hate.

"*Sapristi!*" he gasped. "That little Crosby rat—I told 'Reste not to trust him! Just because we didn't get the Deming diamond, he thought we were holding out on him—and he squealed."

Desperately, he tried to raise himself, to get to his feet; but his strength was gone. His muscles went limp, and he slumped back inertly to the floor, while tears of rage filmed his glaring eyes.

"That dirty rat!" he snarled. "If I could only get over to the Savoy... If I could only get my hands on his throat...."

Wentworth waited for no more. Allen Crosby was the man he wanted, and Allen Crosby was at the Savoy, probably lining up fresh victims to be handed over to Oreste Galento and his killers. Allen Crosby... Wentworth's hands balled into fists, and the last drop of compassion drained out of his heart. Allen Crosby was even lower than these killers, a treacherous Judas for whom the electric chair was too good....

Hurrying through the excited crowd of patrons and employees, Wentworth and Jackson reached the rear of the Armageddon, went through the deserted kitchen and pantries and out through the back door. From there they worked their way to the rear of the theater next door and came out through the alley on its far side, safely on the street as the police were swarming into the night-club and locking its doors.

Grimly, Wentworth strode into the Savoy Club to confront the finger-man. At first, it seemed that Crosby was not there, but then he spied the youth—sitting in a booth deep in conversation with the blonde Renee Wilson. Wentworth started toward them.

It was the entertainer who saw him coming. He saw her whisper something to young Crosby. The youth glanced up quickly, his face paling. For a moment, he seemed too panic-stricken to move. Frantically, his eyes darted around the place—then suddenly he bolted from the table for a corridor that led toward the rear of the establishment.

Wentworth quickened his step, reached the corridor a moment later, just in time to see him racing toward a flight of stairs. At the foot, Crosby whirled and stood quaking with fear.

"Stay back!" he warned wildly. "Don't make me kill you!" Out of his pocket came an automatic. "Stay back or I'll shoot—"

Wentworth dived low. The automatic roared twice. Bullets sped past him wildly—and then Crosby was racing up the steps, sprinting along the upper hall to a rear window, tugging it open, climbing out.

There was a narrow ledge running along beneath that window, barely wide enough for a toehold. A sure-footed man might have been able to cling to it, but Crosby had not gone two steps before his foot slipped, threshed in the air as he tried to hold on with his hands—and then he was tumbling head over heels, down into the courtyard two stories below.

Wentworth heard the sickening crack as his skull hit the stone pavement, heard his gasping moan... and when he reached the courtyard Crosby was barely conscious. A fractured skull, the ambulance intern pronounced; but at the hospital it was discovered that his neck was broken as well—that he had only minutes to live.

COMMISSIONER KIRKPATRICK was there with Wentworth at young Crosby's bedside when he died. Just before life left him he managed to open his eyes, move his lips and barely whisper.

"I knew—that *you* knew—as soon as I saw you tonight." He looked into Wentworth's eyes as he struggled for breath. "I did it—I gave the tip on Deming. But I didn't think... there would be any killing. I worked with them before—half a dozen times—without that. I had to... had to have money... had to get it no matter...."

That was all, but it was plenty for Stanley Kirkpatrick.

"There you are," he exulted. "There is the fingerman I knew

we would find. He has been at the bottom of this whole baffling crime wave. With his contacts, he was able to open the doors wide to Galento's mob. Now that he is dead there will be an end to these mysterious robberies and suicides."

Wentworth eyed him keenly, and wondered whether he really believed that—or whether he was voicing what he desperately hoped was true. Kirk might be convinced, but he was not. He believed young Crosby's confession, and thought that probably his son's guilt had been held over Gilbert Crosby's head as a weapon to force him to rob his customers—but that did not explain a good many of the recent crimes and their peculiar aftermaths....

In the midst of Kirkpatrick's jubilation he was called to the telephone. When Wentworth met him in the corridor, he came back white-faced and crestfallen.

"Frank Lochridge is dead," he said dully. "He killed his wife and committed suicide."

Lochridge, the subway contractor, was one of the commissioner's best friends. When Wentworth looked into Kirkpatrick's haggard eyes, he saw that the commissioner was no longer trying to deceive himself. The reign of terror was not over, and he knew it. All that they had reached in the death of Allen Crosby was the end of a branch stream, while the mad main current of crime raged on unchecked.

"It has gotten so that we don't know whom to trust, Dick," he said bitterly. "Frank Lochridge—he never had a serious quarrel with Ellen that I knew of—they were always perfectly happy. But he put two bullets through her head. Who will be next?

Anyone. Anyone of the friends we shake hands with tonight may be a thief and a murderer in the morning!"

He shook his head. "The thing is uncanny, Dick. My best men are absolutely at sea because they are confronted with crime that doesn't make sense—with a type of crime and criminal with which they have had no experience. A type of over-night criminal with which *nobody* has had any experience—"

Abruptly his train of thought seemed to stop, and he looked squarely at the tall, well set-up, strongly handsome man at his side. He stared shrewdly into Wentworth's keenly alert eyes, and perhaps tried to fathom what was going on in the tireless brain behind them.

"Perhaps I should not say 'nobody,'" he retracted. "The Spider seems to have combatted every type of criminal. Even though, under ordinary circumstances, I do not approve his methods, if there ever was a time when he could be of help to me—this it is. Yes—" he nodded slowly—"this is once when I am willing to admit that I *need* the Spider."

Man to man, those two old friends faced each other—and in the mind of each that statement echoed and reechoed.

Kirkpatrick was a man of law and order, who hewed to the line of his code and would countenance no infraction of the law even though the law itself was served by that liberty which was taken with it. Wentworth, lone crusader against crime in high places and low, had just as high a respect for the law. But he did not feel that the best interests of society were served when its servants were bound by red tape and restrictions which put them at the mercy of the unfettered crooks and racketeers whose cunning placed them out of ordinary reach.

Kirkpatrick disapproved of the Spider, not for what he accomplished but for the means he used to that end, and as police commissioner of New York City he was sworn to apprehend and jail him if ever he could discover his identity. For that, Wentworth held him no grudge. In fact, had Kirkpatrick been otherwise, he could not have retained the respect and genuine regard Wentworth held for him.

In his innermost mind, Stanley Kirkpatrick shrewdly suspected that Richard Wentworth and the Spider were one. But he had never been able to prove that, even though several times he had come very close to it.

"This is a time when the Spider might be of real service," he repeated deliberately; "a time when I would welcome his help. But, if I am able to discover his identity, our truce will be over the moment this case is finished."

A bid for help from a man who was at his wit's end—but with it a veiled warning that, by accepting such help, he made no compromise with his own principles. Wentworth understood every delicate nuance of that bid—and heard in it a call for help from one of his best friends.

The Spider would answer that call, he promised mutely. But at that moment, when his most likely clue had just frittered away into nothing more than a petty offshoot of the criminal organization that was throttling the city's social and financial leaders, he seemed as far from the solution as Kirkpatrick's newest rookie cop.

CHAPTER 6
EVIL OUT OF THE EAST

DESPITE HIS momentary dejection, Wentworth sensed that he had been within reach of the solution, but had muffed it. Almost, it seemed as if he had had the answer in his hand and had let it slip through his fingers. But how had this happened?

Carefully, he tried to relive the events of the past few hours—the battle in the Armageddon, Salvatore Tresca's dying revelation, his entrance into the Savoy Club and discovery of young Crosby... Subconsciously, he had noticed a dark-skinned face turned in his direction, as he walked toward Crosby's booth. That must have been Gooja Singh—the Hindu had been one of the first to appear at his side when he knelt beside Crosby's broken body in the back yard. Wentworth remembered the glimpse of the man's eyes he had caught—how they seemed to glow with satisfaction when the ambulance intern pronounced young Crosby's death sentence....

And then there were those disjointed, half-articulated sentences which had gasped from Allen Crosby's lips before he lapsed into unconsciousness. He had muttered something about a "her," something about it being "all her fault for blabbing...."

Her? Wentworth's thoughts flashed to Renee Wilson. There was a lead! Renee Wilson seemed to have been much more than casually friendly with young Crosby. The way she had whispered a warning of Wentworth's approach would seem to indicate that she knew what was about to happen. Perhaps she knew what

Crosby had been doing. Perhaps she had squealed, or had merely talked too freely....

When the Savoy Club closed early that morning Wentworth was in a cab across the street, waiting patiently for Renee Wilson to appear. She came out alone and hailed a taxi, was driven across town and to a block in the East Sixties. As she stepped to the door and rang the bell, Wentworth's cab started down the block—was just passing when the door opened and she was admitted. She was admitted by a brown-faced doorman wearing a turban!

Again Wentworth had come upon a Hindu trail. But this time he would not walk blindly into their hands.

Four doors down the street was an apartment building no higher than its neighbors. The hall lock responded to the first skeleton key he tried, and then his way was clear to the roof. Carefully, he picked his footing over the housetops until he reached the building Renee Wilson had entered.

There was no fire-escape. But out from beneath his vest came

a thin, strong silken rope—a trusty strand of the Spider's web that had served him well on many an occasion. Fastening it securely to the coping, he let himself down, hand over hand, to the floor below, swung there until he got a foothold on the windowsill. The room behind the pane was dark and silent. Warily, he played the beam of his pencil flashlight into the narrow space beside the drawn shade and found that the room was unfurnished.

Carving a hole in the pane with his glass-cutter, he climbed inside and tiptoed to the door. Beyond that was a hall, dark and silent, with a spiral staircase close at hand. At the head of the stairs, he paused and listened, caught what seemed to be the murmur of voices from below. Cautiously, he started down-ward; passed two floors—and now the voices were much louder, almost distinguishable.

This floor was rigged up like the interior of an Oriental palace. Rugs, tapestries and drapes covered the walls, and dim light came from stained-glass lanterns. The stairway he had been using was the rear one. From it a corridor led toward the front of the house—and from that direction came the low buzz of conversation.

Wentworth listened. That was Renee Wilson's voice, shrill with excitement as the words rushed from her lips.

"He went out of his head," she was saying. "He shook so that he could hardly stand up. Then he ran out of the booth and tried to get away—ran upstairs instead of down into the cellar."

That was Allen Crosby she was talking about. So she had hurried here to give an account of his death the moment she was free? Then this, no doubt, was where she had done the "blabbing" that young Crosby had blamed for his undoing....

Wentworth parted the curtains at the end of the corridor and cat-footed into it. He started forward noiselessly on the heavy-pile rug—but when he reached the other end he found that there was no doorway. The corridor was a blind alley that terminated against a solid wall... and yet those voices were there somewhere very close to him.

Puzzled, he turned and started back to the curtained opening—only to find that it had disappeared! The end of the corridor through which he had entered was now like the other—a dead end that terminated against a blank wall. Carefully, he ran his fingers along that wall, feeling for an opening, for some way of pushing it back where it had come from. But it was solid and immovable.

Glancing behind him, he felt a chill trickle down his spine. That other end of the corridor was much closer to him than it had been—and it was coming closer, *creeping* up on him! The side walls, too, were closer together. As he watched incredulously he saw that they were slowly converging; and that the ceiling was also coming down!

Vainly, he beat against those solid walls. Like a man in a nightmare he ran from end to end of the narrowing corridor, but there was no escape. He was trapped, and the trap was closing inexorably. Closer and closer the walls and ceiling came—so close that he was forced to his knees; so close that his elbows touched both sides. Now there wasn't room to kneel. The ceiling was pushing down on his shoulders, threatening to snap his spine unless he lay down flat.

The ends of the corridor were hardly more than six feet apart, the sides less than three.

This was the end. If that press closed any more tightly, he would be squeezed to death, pulped between the converging walls. Desperately, he tugged loose an automatic and fired until the clip was empty. But that only filled his narrow prison with choking fumes. Then his arm was forced down to his side so that he lay in a virtual strait-jacket....

Grimly, he clenched his teeth and waited for the down-pressing ceiling to crack his ribs and cave in his chest. But at that moment the side walls were gone and strong hands seized his arms and legs. Noiselessly, the ceiling rose, and he was dragged to his feet, now held securely by four Oriental-clad Hindus, while a fifth disarmed him.

UNCEREMONIOUSLY, THEY dragged him down the length of the reshaped corridor and into a room where a man in the lavish robes of an Indian potentate sat regarding him sardonically.

"So you thought to call upon the Swami Rastra without an appointment?" the fellow mocked, while Wentworth stared at the gold mask that covered the upper half of his face. "That we cannot permit—and have taken precautions to prevent. Perhaps in the morning I shall have time to hear the reason for your visit—but not tonight, Mr. Wentworth!"

At a nod of his turbaned head, the Hindus dragged Wentworth away down another corridor and then into a barred metal cage. This cage was almost the full size of the little room it occupied. A lock snapped shut on the door, and he was a helpless prisoner.

His thoughts were busy with that fellow who called himself Swami Rastra. There was something familiar about the part of his face that was unmasked—something familiar about his voice, even though it was mocking and disguised. Somewhere, Wentworth felt certain, he had met the self-styled swami before… but where?

Could he be Gooja Singh? Perhaps… and yet Wentworth hardly believed that. He felt certain that he would have recognized Gooja Singh. Preston Kendall? The actor was as much at home portraying an Oriental as in his own guise. Perhaps this was the answer to Kendall's mysterious absence from the cast of *The Green Goddess*.…

DISMISSED AFTER Allen Crosby's fatal plunge at the Savoy Club, Jackson had gone home to Sutton Place while Wentworth accompanied the dying youth to the hospital. It was nearly one o'clock, but there was little sleep in the East River stronghold that night. Ram Singh, Wentworth's personal man, and old Jenkyns, the butler, were both waiting for Jackson when he arrived—waiting to hear the outcome of Evelyn Deming's telephone call from the Armageddon.

Wentworth, Jackson, Ram Singh and Jenkyns—those four had been through fire and water together, facing death innumerable times when only their mutual dependability and close cooperation had saved their lives. Between them there was a relationship far different than that of master and servants. Jackson, Ram Singh and Jenkyns served Richard Wentworth not for the sake of their jobs but for the privilege of serving. To each of them he was a man in a million, a friend and leader who deserved and was accorded complete loyalty and devotion.

Gravely, the other two listened to Jackson's recital. Then they divided the remaining hours of the night into watches so that one of them would always be awake beside the telephone in case Wentworth should need aid.

But there was no call that night, and no sign of Wentworth in the morning. Uneasily, Jackson paced the floor as the morning hours slipped by. It was unlike the Major—as he would always regard the man under whom he had served in France—to leave them without word of his whereabouts. That was a sure sign of trouble. And when Nita van Sloan telephoned to ask why Wentworth had not kept his luncheon appointment with her, Jackson knew that his uneasy hunch was well founded.

Morning, afternoon, evening—and still no word. After dinner, Jackson was on the verge of going out and instituting a search when Nita phoned again and asked him to come to her apartment.

Half an hour later, he was facing her, looking into her worried eyes and trying to reassure her.

"Certainly there should have been some word from him," she repeated after Jackson had narrated all that he knew. "I have checked the hospital. He left there with the commissioner. I have checked with Stanley, and he left Dick in front of the building. After that, he simply disappeared. I have even checked with the Crosbys, but they saw nothing of him since he left there yesterday evening."

Silently they faced each other and wondered where to turn next, where to start their search.

The telephone furnished the answer. Nita's eyes brightened, and she leaped up to answer it the moment the bell rang. But as she listened her face clouded, lost its eagerness.

"Miss van Sloan—" a foreign-sounding voice came over the wire—"you do not know who I am so there is no use to give you my name. I have information I believe you desire. Information about the whereabouts of Mr. Richard Wentworth. Does that interest you?"

"Yes—yes; go on." Even in her anxiety Nita kept control of herself while she did her best to place that strange voice.

"Very well," it clipped. "If you will be at the Savoy Club in half an hour, one of my men will meet you there. Leave your table location with the head waiter and my man will come to you."

Before she had a chance to agree or to spar for more time a click on the other end of the line terminated the call. Turning to Jackson, she outlined what she had just heard and eyed him thoughtfully.

"It sounds like a trap," he objected promptly. "You have no way of knowing where this fellow may take you."

"Nevertheless, I am going," she decided firmly. "These people, whoever they are, at least know something."

"The Major would not like it," Jackson frowned. "He would never consent to letting you keep such an appointment alone. He would...."

What Wentworth would have done under such conditions, Jackson knew it was now up to him to do. Gradually, a plan began to take shape in his mind. He outlined this to Nita. At first, she was dubious, but finally he convinced her and they started making their preparations....

HALF AN hour later, Nita van Sloan sat at a table in the Savoy Club and covertly eyed each new arrival ushered into the room. Lone men were few, and none of them came near her—until a dark-skinned Oriental approached her table and bowed obsequiously. A Hindu undoubtedly, which accounted for the unusual accent of that voice on the phone.

"Miss van Sloan," he said softly, "if you are ready I have a car waiting to take you to the Swami Rastra."

There was another Hindu at the wheel of the sedan, Nita noted, as she stepped in. Without a word, he shifted the machine into gear and they started across town. In the tip of the rear-view mirror, she saw that a brown coupé had started away from the curb almost at the same time—and it was running along beside a taxicab behind them.

Over to Fifth Avenue and then uptown to a street in the Sixties, the dark-skinned chauffeur drove. They stopped in front of a four-story brown-stone building with a flight of steps leading up to the second floor doorway. Politely her guide handed her out of the car—then stood waiting at the foot of the steps while she went back to the sedan to recover her handkerchief left on the seat.

When she reached the steps the second time, the brown coupé was gliding up to the curb. The moment it stopped the driver's door opened—and out stepped a man who would have been taken anywhere for Richard Wentworth!

Quickly, he leaped to the side of the sedan and jammed a gun into the neck of the surprised Hindu at the wheel, dragged him from the seat and frisked him for weapons. At the same instant, the handkerchief which Nita had recovered flipped back from the barrel of an automatic that ground into the ribs of her deferential escort.

Shepherding the chauffeur over to the steps, the disguised Jackson held both Hindus under the watchful muzzle of his gun while Nita whispered into his ear and then stepped into her coupé and drove away.

"Okay," he clipped. "Now we're ready for that interview."

Docilely, they climbed the steps ahead of him and rang the bell—with his warning that a bullet would reward their least attempt to trick him. A brown-skinned doorman answered the summons, and stared wide-eyed as Jackson's gun pressed into his belly.

"Inside," the amazing visitor ordered. "We're going in to see your boss. Get moving!"

The doorman's eyes glinted malignantly, but he said no word. Obediently, he turned and led the procession to a large room in the center of the house. Here an elaborately dressed Hindu, with a gold mask over the upper half of his face, awaited them. Even behind that mask Jackson could see his eyes widen with surprise as his men marched in and stood helpless before him.

"I thought I'd better bring these fellows into you before something happens to them." Jackson nodded derisively to the stony-faced Hindus. "They were quite unnecessary, Swami Rastra. When you want to talk with Richard Wentworth it isn't necessary to attempt such a crude decoy to get him to your house. I am here of my own choice—and Miss van Sloan has been sent home, where she belongs."

"Richard Wentworth?" Despite his effort, the swami could not conceal his surprise. "So you are Richard Wentworth?"

"At your service." Jackson half-bowed, and his voice was mocking—but his automatic did not veer from the man in the chair.

"That is very odd." Swami Rastra eyed him with crafty suspicion. "I was under the impression that I was already entertaining Mr. Wentworth before your arrival; yet I never heard that Richard Wentworth had a twin. Perhaps you would like to meet your other self."

He had not moved a finger or given any signal that Jackson had been able to detect—but suddenly the wall hangings parted in three different places, and through the apertures poked revolvers that covered Jackson's heart. The face beneath the mask twisted into a smile, the eyes mocked him.

Jackson's gun did not waver. "Okay," he clipped icily. "Tell them to blaze away, Rastra—but before I go down you will have at least two bullets in your brain."

"Perhaps you are Richard Wentworth," the masked man conceded with grudging admiration. "If you are, put away your gun and my men will holster theirs. You have my word. That display was only to reveal to you how useless your own weapon would have been had I wanted to have you killed."

Jackson accepted that bargain. He slipped the automatic into its shoulder holster, and the threatening revolvers drew back through the slits that closed over them.

"That is much better," Swami Rastra nodded. "If you are Richard Wentworth, we should work together—not *against* each other. But first let me introduce you to your double."

WITH JACKSON at his side, he led the way to the room where Wentworth sat in his steel-barred cage. Jackson's pulses leaped when that door opened, but he showed not the smallest surprise. Not the slightest flicker betrayed the deception to the watchful eyes of the swami. Instead, he grinned deprecatingly at the prisoner.

"Still at it, eh, flatfoot?" he jeered. "You must get a lot of fun out of playing Richard Wentworth. But the way you handle the job isn't very flattering to me. Take the way you're sitting there now, for example. I think I'll have to ask the commissioner to assign someone to my role who's a bit more careful."

Contemptuously, he turned away.

"This fellow is one of Commissioner Kirkpatrick's men," he told the sharp-eyed swami. "He has been posing as me for a long time—uses the masquerade to get in where he could not penetrate otherwise. Now it seems that he has himself in deeper than he intended."

"A masquerader?" The masked man nodded. "Masqueraders are a nuisance—we know how to dispose of them effectively. He will trouble you no more, Mr. Wentworth."

Jackson's eyes narrowed and his face lost its tolerant grin, became hard and sneering, as he turned back to the cage.

"On second thought," he hazarded desperately, "I have had enough of this fellow's interference. I will attend to him, myself."

"Very good—that is your privilege," the swami's suave voice endorsed readily. "Now is an excellent time. My men will go with you to be sure there is no—er, slip-up."

Jackson felt like a mouse in the claws of a cat. This Swami Rastra could have had both Wentworth and him murdered—but for some reason chose, instead, to play this subtle game. Instead of a killing here in the house, he was to take Wentworth out and despatch him. These dark-skinned henchmen would have plenty of weapons when they accompanied him on that murder mission. But at least the odds should be better outside than penned up in this trap....

One of the Hindus unlocked the cage, and two others stood ready to seize Wentworth when he stepped out. Out to the sedan they led him, to thrust him into the back and then bow Jackson in beside him. Two of them crowded into the rear and two more occupied the front seat.

They were taking no chance whatever on a "slip-up," Jackson observed. He debated his chance of making a desperate draw and fighting it out with the four of them. They would kill him, of course, but in the struggle in that tightly crowded car Wentworth might be able to get his hands on a gun and battle his way clear.

With three alert-eyed Hindus watching Jackson's every move, the chance of success was about one in a thousand. But it seemed the only hope, until he felt the muscle of Wentworth's arm flex at his side—a *series* of flexes. There they were again—*the SOS in Morse code!*

Jackson nodded, and then concentrated all attention on the message coming over that muscle-telegraph.

"Fine," he read the flexes. *"Keep it up. Pretend to kill me. Go on being me. I will bring help."*

The car had headed across town and was turning north, swinging into Riverside Drive. Soon the driver cut down the speed, and Jackson knew that the test was close at hand. He steeled his nerves and waited until the Hindus had found a spot to their liking. The driver swung in a U-turn and drew up at the curb.

"This is an admirable place," the fellow who sat beside the driver said softly. "Kill him and throw him over the edge."

Jackson's automatic was in his hand, jammed into Wentworth's ribs as he backed out of the car.

"Out—you," he commanded gruffly. The gun muzzle stayed close, swung around to Wentworth's back. They marched across the path and stepped over the low fence to the edge of the hill, with the snaky-eyed Hindus watching on all sides, alert for the first sign of treachery.

The edge of the hill, then the gun roared—not more than two inches from Wentworth's kidney! So close that they could smell the odor of scorched cloth. With a groan of pain, Wentworth clutched at his back, strained up on his toes—and then all the strength seemed to flow out of him. His knees buckled and he toppled headlong, pitched down the steep hill in an avalanche of dirt and stones. Jackson sent three more bullets lancing after him.

For a moment longer, the noise of that rolling, tumbling descent came back to them. Then, abruptly, it ceased—and they knew that he had reached the sheer edge of the bluff.

Poker-faced and sneering, Jackson stood there peering down into the darkness, but cold fear clutched at his heart. Had Wentworth been able to break his fall? Was that sudden quiet really as ominous as it sounded…?

"And now, if you will please let me have that weapon." The soft-voiced leader of the Hindus was at his side with a leveled revolver held ready. "You will be supplied with another to replace it," he assured as he pocketed Jackson's automatic, "but Swami Rastra desires to keep this one—as a souvenir."

As a threat to hold over his head—that was why Swami Rastra wanted that murder gun, Jackson understood quickly. While the swami held the weapon from which the bullets had been fired into that supposedly murdered corpse, his word would be law and Richard Wentworth would do as he was told under threat of being turned over to the police as a cop-killer….

WENTWORTH LAY flat on the ground, straining ears and eyes as he peered up the hill. He waited until the dark shapes at its crest had disappeared, and he thought he heard the Hindus' machine starting away from the curb. Jackson had gotten off with it beautifully—thanks to his habit of carrying his automatic on a blank cartridge. Swami Rastra would think that the impostor was dead, and would be totally unprepared for the raid that would spell the end of him and his gang.

Painfully, Wentworth crawled out from beneath the clump of bushes that had stopped his landsliding fall just when it seemed to be out of control. Warily, he climbed back to the top of the steep grade and assured himself that the swami's men really had gone. Brushing off his disheveled clothing as well as possible, he stepped out, hailed a taxi, ordered the driver to take him to the nearest telephone.

"I have your man, Kirk—the one who was behind Allen Crosby," he announced the moment he routed the police commissioner out of bed. "He is a Swami Rastra, the head of a Hindu outfit. He tried to have me murdered tonight and is now holding my man, Jackson, a prisoner."

"Where?" Kirkpatrick barked excitedly. "The address, man!"

Wentworth supplied it, and then hurried back to his waiting cab. By the time he reached the swami's headquarters, the block was already swarming with police cars. The officers had surrounded the house and were covering it from front and rear. Under Kirkpatrick's personal supervision, they now charged through the door at the head of the high stoop and battered in the windows of the lower floor—only to come back outside like a lot of schoolboys who had fallen for an April Fool joke.

"There's nobody in there," the captain of the raiders reported disgustedly. "The place is empty. Must be the wrong address."

But Wentworth was already past him, sprinting up the steps and into that front hallway where he had last seen Swami Rastra smiling sardonically as Jackson led him out to his supposed death. The rugs and draperies were all gone from the walls; the carpet had vanished from the floor. The place was entirely bare.

Room after room, all were the same, all empty—and so devoid of the slightest sign of recent occupancy that even the dust lay undisturbed on the floor!

CHAPTER 7
WHILE THE IRON IS HOT

AS RICHARD WENTWORTH tramped through those empty, echoing rooms, he could almost have believed that Swami Rastra was possessed of supernatural powers. Every sign of his establishment had been whisked away as if by magic. Wentworth was left in the role of leader of a wild-goose chase—to explain to the skeptical police how a house full of furniture could have vanished in little more than an hour's time.

Even Stanley Kirkpatrick looked dubious. But for the evidence of the top-floor rear window pane, with the hole he had cut in it, Wentworth might have thought that in some inconceivable way he had become confused in the address.

But there was no mistake—this was the house. Swami Rastra's swift disappearance, with all his belongings, was easily explained. Probably only one floor of the house had been furnished—and that with equipment that could quickly be removed. Once convinced that he had the actual Richard Wentworth in his hands, the cagey swami had flown—for fear that Wentworth might have made forehanded preparations for his rescue in case he did not return promptly.

Swami Rastra's establishment was gone—but there was another Hindu layout that might not have had time to evaporate. Gooja Singh's! Wentworth was convinced that both were part of the same criminally directed organization.

Gooja Singh's was the place to go! If the Hindus were convinced that they had Richard Wentworth in their hands, they would not be expecting interference from him now. This was the time to strike!

As soon as he could get away from Kirkpatrick, Wentworth hailed a taxi and was driven to a side-street address near the West Side waterfront. The dark alley, into which he disappeared, led to a ramshackle wooden building that had once been a livery stable but was now broken up into a number of small private garages.

Unlocking one of these, he stepped inside and turned on the cowl lights of what appeared to be an ordinary, second-hand coupé. But the looks of that machine were deceiving—they gave no indication of the capacious pockets concealed behind its sides and seat cushions—or suggestion of the possibilities of its high-speed motor. This was one of the emergency cars he kept cached in widely scattered parts of the city.

Out from the compartment behind the seat came a change of clothing, and a pair of automatics to replace those Swami Rastra's men had taken. Speedily, his fingers went to work before a little makeup mirror, and once more the face that was Richard Wentworth's began to disappear. When he drove out of that alleyway, a few minutes later, it was a dignified, brown-skinned Hindu, with a trim black mustache and a tightly wound turban over his glistening blue-black hair, who sat at the wheel.

Straight to Gooja Singh's residence he drove, parked the

car on the corner and approached the building on foot. As he expected, a light still burned dimly in the hallway. Boldly, he approached the door and rang the bell—to be admitted promptly by a Hindu servant who seemed to be expecting arrivals at that hour of the morning.

THE DEVIL'S CANDLESTICKS

He hurled Gooja Singh's body over the edge
to land in front of the burning building!

He stepped back to let the newcomer enter. Before he had time to realize his mistake, Wentworth was at his throat, cutting off his breath so that he could not yell, pounding him into swift unconsciousness with an automatic barrel.

Dragging the fellow to one side of the hall, and stretching him out in the deep shadow of the staircase, Wentworth started down the corridor. He headed for that room in which he had had his previous interview with Gooja Singh. There were voices emanating from it now—Gooja Singh's and those of several others, speaking a mixture of Indian dialects and English.

A little room just beyond the main audience chamber proved to be just what Wentworth needed. It opened onto the larger room, and the connecting door stood partially open. He could see into the place. Gooja Singh was seated at a small desk, with a book spread open before him. Squatting on the floor in front of him were four imposingly arrayed Orientals, while several servants stood in the background.

"THIS RANDOLPH woman is an excellent lead," Gooja Singh was saying as he made a notation in his record book. "She has splendid connections and should open to us the private coffers of half the Claybilt family. Excellent work, my dear Sutra Nahr, excellent work!"

One of the squatting Hindus shrugged.

"She is a credulous fool," he grinned. "It was so easy to convince her that I, the seventh son of a seventh son, have private access to all the wisdom of the universe. Now she is sure that I can straighten out her nasty little love intrigues before they reach the ears of her husband. But, of course, to do that I must know everything—*everything!*"

His jeering voice ended in a sardonic chuckle, as Gooja Singh turned to one of the others. Wentworth, listening, learned more and more of the amazing inner workings of the despicable racket this Hindu outfit was conducting....

Those four on the floor were crystal-gazers who were doing business in various parts of the city—all employees of Gooja Singh, or of Swami Rastra, his superior. They were only a few of the score or more, all engaged in operating a huge blackmail scheme that was based on the ill-advised confidences these fake clairvoyants wrung from the lips of their unsuspecting victims! Moving in the best of social circles, they were choosing their clients with fine discrimination—craftily undermining those on whom the social and financial structure of the city depended!

A diabolically vicious criminal set-up that must be netting its masters millions of dollars!

One after the other, those squatting fakers reported damning confidences pried from the trusting lips of simple-minded women; intimate confidences that would be held over their own heads and used to bully their husbands and lovers into doing almost anything to keep those shameful indiscretions from being made public!

Gooja Singh's place was the clearing-house for this filthy cargo of gossip and confession. Here his "mystics" came to report and to be supplied with new lists of victims who were to be solicited and tricked into paying them a visit. Dozens of familiar names—names of his friends, of some of the city's most respected women—Wentworth heard dealt out to those human leeches. Then one of them brought up the name of Milo Spencer, the scourge of their kind.

That name stirred an immediate storm of snarling curses.

"He is a poisonous adder, that man." The fellow who was called Sutra Nahr spat vindictively. "He spies on me continually and will never believe the amounts I report to him."

"Cease to worry about Milo Spencer." Gooja Singh soothed them with a significant smile. "He will trouble you no longer. He has been assigned to young Wesley Brewster who will—"

His voice sank lower, and Wentworth pressed close to the edge of the door, strained to hear. But at that moment the doorbell rang loudly—two long, rasping peals. A moment or two of silence, and then the summons was repeated, longer and more insistently.

Gooja Singh looked up in surprise, but Wentworth had already started to retrace his footsteps. Unless he could reach that door, and open it before one of the other servants was sent to answer the bell, the doorman's absence would be discovered and investigated. Back into the corridor, he padded softly. But as he passed the main door of Gooja Singh's audience room, one of the Hindus almost collided with him.

Instantly, Wentworth was upon the fellow, had him by the throat and was forcing him back, away from that door and toward the front of the hall. But the man was wiry, strong. He corded his neck, did his best to shout for help, while his right hand plucked at his waist and flashed back with a sharp-pointed dagger gripped for a downward plunge.

Wentworth captured his wrist just in time, held onto it grimly while his other hand tightened on the fellow's windpipe. Like two statues, almost immovable but straining with every ounce of strength in their lithe, well muscled bodies, they stood there. Gradually, the Hindu began to weaken. Panic-stricken realization of defeat flared in his eyes, and his tongue protruded thickly from his gasping mouth… but at that moment the bell rang again. Now the impatient new arrival kept his finger on the button!

OUT FROM Gooja Singh's room poked a brown-skinned face. Dark eyes popped wide with amazement—and then the fellow was frantically yelling an alarm. It brought the whole outfit surging out of the audience room, just as Wentworth's struggling adversary heaved himself away from the wall in a last desperate effort to break loose.

For an instant, they teetered off-balance and then tumbled to the floor. Silence no longer possible, Wentworth's steely fingers loosened their hold on the brown throat. His fist smashed into the gasping face, as his other hand wrenched the knife out of the fellow's weakening fingers. Before the released Hindu could scramble clear, his own dagger plunged deep into his throat— then was raised again, to speed like a bullet at the pack surging down the hall.

Seizing the dying man, and holding him up as a shield, Wentworth unholstered one of his automatics and poured a deadly fire into that brown-skinned horde. Two of the fake mystics screamed and sprawled headlong. Then the rest were upon

Wentworth, stabbing at him with their knives, as he battered his guns into their faces.

That punishment was too much for them. Panting, cursing, they gave ground before this man who seemed to be invincible—and the moment they were clear leaden death cut them down once more. Behind them, Gooja Singh was screaming orders in Hindustani—calling them pigs and yellow cowards, threatening to kill them himself if they did not prove that they were men.

Stung by those taunts, fearful of the threat at their backs, they came on again.

Wentworth sprang to meet them, lashed out savagely with his bloodied weapons. But they crashed full-tilt into him, drove him back, down to his knees—then ran past, racing wildly toward the front door. Two reached it and dived through the portal before he could bring them down. Then he whirled to face Gooja Singh, as the man came leaping at him with knife upraised.

Back and forth across the narrow hall they struggled, Wentworth's automatic pressed down hard against the blade, forcing it back, preventing the murderous-eyed Hindu from getting it loose. Savagely, his fist pounded into the snarling brown face—came up in a smashing uppercut that catapulted Gooja Singh backward and pitched him through the doorway into the room he had just left.

Before he could get to his feet, Wentworth was after him, driving thudding blows into his face. Twice that razor-sharp blade sliced into his arm, but at last he secured a grip on the fellow's wrist and twisted it backward. He twisted until the bones threatened to snap.

The knife-blade was flat against the carpet, as Gooja Singh vainly tried to break that grip. His hand twisted around, the knife-point came steadily upward—and Wentworth stared down at the third finger twisted around the hilt. An opal ring should have encircled that finger. Now it was gone, but clearly marked in the flesh was the place where it had been worn for many years.

So it *was* Gooja Singh who had tried to kidnap Anice Crosby when she came home from her father's funeral!

The Hindu must have read his doom in Wentworth's hard, narrow-slitted eyes, the grim expression of his tight-lipped mouth.

"Let me go!" he pleaded desperately. "I will pay you anything you ask! Let me go—before it is too late! Unless we get out of here at once, we will both die! That is the truth! I am not lying—"

But Wentworth twisted him over farther and farther, arced his writhing body—and relentlessly forced it down onto the point of his own knife that stood upright from the floor!

That house was deathly still, as Gooja Singh's dying breath sobbed from his lips. Panting, Wentworth got to his knees, reached into his coat pocket and then stooped over the dead man's sweat-beaded forehead to press against it the bottom of a silver cigarette-lighter.

When his hand came away, a crimson spider was emblazoned on the brown skin—a warning to the fellow's master and all the rest of his despicable blackmailing outfit that the Spider was close on their trail and that the doom he meted out was inescapable!

HARDLY HAD that crimson insignia blazed forth than the house trembled under a series of ground-shaking explosions. Wentworth heard ceilings falling, plaster dropping from the walls, beams cracking and groaning—and then the lights went out. Springing up from beside the corpse, he ran to a window—only to find that a solid steel plate had slid out from one side of the casing and sealed the opening from top to bottom!

Not only one window, but everyone in the house! The same was true of the door. The building had been sealed so tightly that he could not get out, and nobody could get in from the outside! It had become a trap. When he caught a glimpse of the fire that was licking out from a room at the rear, he understood.

Swami Rastra, or whoever owned that building, was taking no chances that its secrets might fall into the hands of the police.

Ingeniously, the place had been fitted with batter-proof steel shutters which would hold the firemen at bay until the interior was a raging inferno in which every bit of incriminating evidence had been consumed.

That was what Gooja Singh had meant about dying together in the house. He had known that the destroying mechanism was in operation. Undoubtedly, Gooja Singh was the lieutenant in that murderous organization, but, even though he was dead, Swami Rastra, the leader, was still alive. And those of his men who had escaped through the front door must have doomed the building before they left.

Picking his way with his flashlight, through the piles of debris, Wentworth ran from floor to floor. But every way of escape seemed to be blocked. The fire, which had broken out in a dozen different places, was spreading with appalling speed. Nowhere was there an exit that he could force—until he reached the top floor. The roof-house door was sealed like the rest, but the kiosk-like structure was made of wood—that did not seem very substantial. Dragging up to it chairs, lamps, anything that was not too heavy to wield, he battered away at the flimsy siding until it splintered. Then he was able to get a purchase on the broken boards, tear them loose and rip a hole sufficiently large to crawl through.

Inside the building the flames were roaring, the smoke billowing in great, suffocating clouds. But Wentworth dived back down the stairs to the room where Gooja Singh's body lay. Lifting the corpse over his shoulder, he panted his way back to the roof. He fought doggedly upward although it seemed that his lungs must collapse under the terrific strain and the scorching smoke that seared them.

After an eternity of agony, he staggered out onto the roof and dragged Gooja Singh's body after him—hauled it to the coping and pushed it over the edge so that it would land in front of the door four floors below. Even though the building burned to the ground, Wentworth wanted that body to be found. He wanted the masked-faced swami to hear of that brand on his lieutenant's forehead, and know that the Spider had escaped from the holocaust to bring grim retribution stalking close on his heels!

Halfway down the block, Wentworth found a roof-scuttle that opened when he tugged at it. A few minutes later he was back on the street, steering his coupé around the corner, as fire apparatus converged on the block from every direction.

It was close to four o'clock, but Wentworth's destination was the home of Milo Spencer. Unless he had misconstrued Gooja Singh's meaning, the old man was in grave danger—if he had not already paid for his interference with the smooth working of the Hindu blackmail ring.

THE BLOCK was deserted when his coupé turned into it—absolutely empty except for a sedan parked without lights a few doors from Spencer's residence. The house was dark, and there was no response when he rang persistently. No sign of life inside—and yet he was almost certain that he had heard a sound beyond that door just as his finger touched the bell button the first time....

Carefully, he tried his skeleton keys, found one that fitted, and opened the door, warily. Utter stillness inside—but there was a light burning in Spencer's office at the rear. Wentworth's hair seemed to stand on end as he sensed the presence of some-one close at hand.

Quickly, he stepped through the doorway and closed it behind him, as his hand flashed to his shoulder-holstered auto-matic. But before he could draw the weapon, something leaped at him from the darkness and a ton weight seemed to crash down on his head. Groggily, he staggered back, and then was hurled against the wall with stunning force.

The world spun crazily around him, as he tried to grab onto something to hold himself upright. For an instant, someone bent close over him—a dark-skinned face that he recognized instantly. Preston Kendall made up for his role as the Indian prince in *The Green Goddess!*

But Kendall wasn't really leaning over him; he was stooping to pick up something from the floor—the limp body of a white-faced man with familiar curly hair. Kendall had him in his arms, was carrying him through the doorway out into the street. Wentworth caught only a blurred glimpse of the unconscious man's face....

Then they were gone.

Pulling himself to his feet, he yanked the door open. But the parked car was already in motion, leaping from the curb and heading toward the avenue. Too late to try to overhaul it now. Instead, Wentworth turned back into the building, walked back to Spencer's office—and stopped, aghast, at the threshold!

The place was a wreck, the big desk ransacked and the safe standing open. There in the middle of the littered floor lay the body of the grafting reformer, his gray head in a widening pool of his own blood! An ugly black hole in his temple bathed his face with the crimson stream, as his dead fingers still clutched at the bankbooks and records that had been his very life.

That was not all. A few feet from Spencer's corpse lay the body of a Hindu with an Oriental-handled knife plunged deep into his chest!

A double murder... Wentworth stared down at the bodies and tried to reconstruct what had happened. Two men had passed him out there at the doorway. One of those he was certain was Preston Kendall—but who was that other, white-faced man he was carrying?

Was it Wesley Brewster? Brewster who had come there with this Hindu to carry out his murderous "assignment" and kill

Spencer? But how had the Hindu met death with his own knife, and where did Preston Kendall come into that setup? Why was he there, and why had he carried Brewster's limp body from the building?

There was no time to stand trying to find the answers in the middle of that blood-spattered room. The police might be along at any moment. This layout had all the earmarks of a frame-up trap, and Wentworth got out of it promptly—just in time to hear the police sirens converging on the block, as he turned into the avenue.

CHAPTER 8
CRYSTAL RACKET

DEATH HAD eliminated Gooja Singh and Milo Spencer from his list of possible suspects, Wentworth considered as he drove uptown. Preston Kendall he could not locate, much as he would have liked to find the fellow—and the whereabouts and identity of Swami Rastra were as much a mystery as ever.

However, the swami held Jackson, and believed that Jackson was Richard Wentworth. That belief must be preserved at all costs, until Jackson could be located and rescued. Any little slip which aroused the swami's suspicions would mean a speedy death for the masquerading chauffeur. Now Wentworth must not risk returning to his own headquarters where he might be seen. Instead, he put the car in a garage and checked in under an assumed name at a quiet midtown hotel.

Dawn was streaking the sky before he got to bed that morning, but by ten o'clock he had telephoned Nita and Ram Singh and asked them to meet him for a conference.

"There is the answer to our crime wave," he concluded his brisk recital of what he had discovered. "This Swami Rastra is running and controlling it with a regiment of fake mystics and Hindu strong-arm men. He had a strangle-hold on the crystal-gazing business in this town. Everyone of these incredible crimes can be traced back to one of these fellows. They drag the information out of some unsuspecting client—then pass it on through Gooja Singh."

He continued. "Gooja Singh is out of business. Swami Rastra is the one we want now. He is the one holding Jackson. The only way to save Jackson is to locate the swami and break up his pack of leeches—"

"That is a task that is rightfully mine, master," Ram Singh's deep voice interrupted, his bearded face bleak with rage. "These dogs are a disgrace to the race that spawned them. I ask nothing more than the privilege of cleansing the earth of their foul presence!"

His dark eyes flashed, and his strong hands clenched on the arms of his chair so that the knuckles stood out whitely through the dark skin. Ram Singh was a man of great pride—pride in himself, his family, his people. The son of a long line of renowned warriors, never had he condescended to serve any man until he met Richard Wentworth—and recognized in him a man deserving of his allegiance and unswerving devotion.

Wentworth's enemies were his enemies, and under his stern

Sikh code enemies received short shrift. But when those enemies were renegades of his own race the hot warrior blood boiled in his veins and his fingers itched to draw the thirsty knife that was his favorite weapon.

"I think you may be able to locate this fellow where I have failed, Ram Singh," Wentworth agreed. "Unless I am mistaken, he and his organization will brook no interference, no competition in the crystal-gazing racket. That is where you come in. If a new mystic opens up shop, they ought to pay him a visit in short order—either to drive him out of town or force him into line. If we can set you up in an establishment, and start a string of wealthy customers going to you, we ought to get action."

"I know where a place of that sort can be secured," the Sikh nodded. "A cinema conception of a Hindu palace. I can engage it within the hour and become a master-mind by this afternoon if the *sahib* wishes."

Carefully, they made their plans, and when that conference was over "Kira Singh" was ready to take his place among the Oriental wise-men who cater to gullible New Yorkers. While Ram Singh attended to engaging and arranging the establishment to his liking, Nita and Wentworth launched a campaign to round up customers for the new mystic. One after the other, Wentworth jotted down the names of the prospective victims Gooja Singh had doled out to his henchmen.

"Concentrate on these," he advised Nita. "That will be like snatching cake right out of the swami's hands—the surest way to gain his attention in a hurry."

That strategy worked perfectly. The second day that Ram

Singh was in business he was visited by two emissaries of the crystal-racket boss. He listened frigidly to their veiled threats and then showed them to the door—while his fingers hovered over the handle of the long knife sheathed in his belt.

The third day they were back again, four of them this time.

"Yesterday you showed little wisdom," the leader rebuked him, as the others gathered around and hemmed him in. "One who was less tolerant than the swami we represent would have given you no second opportunity. But the great swami has compassion on your blindness. Tonight, however, you will be ready to be taken to report to him, or else—"

In a twinkling two of them had seized Ram Singh's arms, while a third whipped a silken garrote around his throat and twisted it tight. Mightily Ram Singh struggled to hold himself in check as those filthy hands dared to defile him, and grimly he promised himself an early reckoning.

"The punishment of Kali," the leader nodded. "Only the graciousness of the swami allows you to escape with your life this time. Be wise and do not try his patience again."

That night a car arrived for him, and he was taken, blind-folded, to make the acquaintance of Swami Rastra.

"We can use you, Kira Singh," the gold-masked swami decided after he had cross-questioned Ram Singh and been given the story Wentworth had outlined. "You seem to be able to attract the right sort of people—the type of clientele with which we want to deal. Continue as you have been doing, but when you are closeted with a client there are certain things we shall expect you to learn."

And then Ram Singh received his instructions. He was told how to pry into the private lives of his clients, win their confidence and work them up to a state of confessional. He was to tabulate the material he secured and have it ready for the swami's collectors.

He was one of the blackmail outfit, he exulted as he listened—things had worked out exactly as Wentworth planned. Now all that remained was to learn the address of this establishment—and the identity of Swami Rastra, who, he knew, was no Hindu.

But the voice of the swami broke in rudely on his satisfaction.

"For a salon such as you must maintain you will need servants," the masked man was saying. "A doorman, one to lead the client to you, another to answer your call when you signal for him. Three of my men will be assigned to you."

Three of Swami Rastra's men—but instead of servants Ram Singh soon found that they were his jailers. Once he returned to his own quarters, he was virtually a prisoner there, guarded and watched so carefully that he could not even get word out to Wentworth or Nita van Sloan.

IT WAS on the evening of Ram Singh's visit to Swami Rastra that Nita van Sloan's telephone rang to announce that Anice Crosby was downstairs in the lobby and would like to see her. Nita knew Anice fairly well, and her heart went out to her in this time of double tragedy. But she was not prepared for the near-hysteria which greeted her the moment Anice entered the apartment.

"I came to you because I have to talk to someone, Miss van Sloan," she cried. "I have tried to reach Mr. Wentworth, but nobody seems to know where he is—unless you can tell me. He tried to help me twice. But I was foolish enough not to let him—lied to him—and now I need him *desperately!*"

"I can't tell you where to find Mr. Wentworth, but perhaps I can help you until we locate him." Nita set about winning her confidence, and soon the girl was pouring out her troubles.

"It's Wesley Brewster—I'm frantic about him," she confessed. "He has disappeared, simply dropped out of sight. He disappeared three nights ago—the night Allen was killed. He didn't even come to Allen's funeral this morning. All that I have had from him is a brief note that said he was all right. But I don't believe it, Miss van Sloan! That note didn't sound like him—I don't believe it! He is in danger, I know! Either he's been hurt or is held prisoner somewhere—nothing else would keep him away from me so long!"

Nita had heard from Wentworth of this girl's peculiar behavior. Now she studied her keenly, convinced that Anice was sincere, and crazed with anxiety.

"Don't worry, we'll locate him," Nita said, and then ventured a question as if it had just occurred to her. "Do you ever consult mystics—crystal-gazers—people who can read the future?"

"No," Anice looked doubtful. "I never had much faith in people like that. But my sister Margaret sometimes goes to a Hindu professor—a man named Sutra Nahr. She seems to think he is quite wonderful."

"In a case like this, we must take advantage of every possible help," Nita decided, grasping at this opportunity to establish connection with the blackmail ring. "It is just possible that this man may be able to aid us. If you can find out where he is located, we might try to see him tonight."

Anice telephoned to her sister and secured the address. Half an hour later, they were at Sutra Nahr's door. Nita hesitated there.

"For this consultation, it will be better if I am—Sally Manning," she told the girl. Then the door opened for them.

The layout was as usual for places of that sort—dim lights and Oriental draperies, a turbaned doorman and warm air that was heavy with the odor of sandalwood. The professor could receive only one at a time, the doorman told them. Anice went in first, while Nita waited on a low divan in the reception room and tried to figure how Sutra Nahr fitted in with Gooja Singh and the mysterious Swami Rastra, the tragedy-stricken Crosbys and, possibly, the missing Wesley Brewster.

Midway in Nita's meditation, Anice came from the consultation room. A glance at the girl's face told that the quite wonderful Sutra Nahr had been unable to perform a miracle for her benefit.

Nita followed the doorman into the rear room and took her seat at one side of the crystal globe as the mystic, tall and stately in his elaborate robes, seated himself opposite her.

"You are in trouble," he began his ritual, as the lights clicked off and the ball began to glow with interior illumination. "You came to Sutra Nahr for help...."

The air in this room was even heavier than in the other, Nita noticed; it made her senses swim. That globe added to her confusion, seeming to throw her eyes out of focus. To rest them for a

110

moment, she raised her glance. The Hindu's dark, compelling eyes were gazing at her, unblinkingly. Words were coming from his barely moving lips, but it was his steady, fathomless eyes that held her—until she realized that the fellow was trying to hypnotize her!

Very well, if that was what he wanted.

Gradually, she let her face become expressionless, her eyes blank and as staring as his own. Now his questions were becoming clearer and more pertinent—questions cunningly prying into her private life under the pretense of securing all available knowledge necessary to "help" her.

"What is it you really want?" he was repeating over and over. "What is the real reason that brings you here? You are no curiosity-seeker. Something vital has brought you to me—something that you want to tell me."

"Yes, there is." Her voice came haltingly at first, and then grew stronger. "I am in trouble—great trouble. I had to have money—a great deal of money. I was desperate to get it. I pretended to have oil-producing property in Oklahoma—which I sold to my friends. I sold it to a dozen of them—more than a hundred thousand dollars' worth. I thought that I would be able to repay them when I married. But now I fear that my fiancé will learn of these sales."

Once she was embarked on the subject, Nita did not stop. Before she was finished, she had confessed complicity in half a dozen crimes that would have made her a social outcast, and headed her for jail, if they were exposed.

At last the session ended, and Nita was escorted back to the reception room where an attendant was serving rose-petal tea. Anice Crosby had already been drinking the fragrant brew, but Nita sniffed hers cautiously. She saw that the girl's eyes were becoming heavy….

Pretending to sip her cup, she took the first opportunity to spill it where it would not be noticed on the rug. Now Anice's eyes were closed, and she was leaning back limply against the wall—and Nita knew that the tea was drugged!

From the doorway, she caught a glimpse of watchful eyes upon her, and for their benefit she pretended to succumb, also. The moment she slumped backward, the Hindus padded softly into the room. One of them picked up Anice Crosby, the other stooped over Nita.

Now was the moment! Frantically, she leaped out of his arms and darted toward the doorway—but another brown-faced husky appeared from nowhere to block her way. Strong arms seized and held her helpless while ropes were lashed around her arms and legs. Then Sutra Nahr was standing over her, grinning down mockingly.

"A very clever masquerade, Miss Nita van Sloan," he laughed, "but unfortunately I was not at all deceived by it. You see, I knew you were coming to see me and was all prepared for you! Yes," he chuckled, "I was very glad to welcome you—for now that you are our guest perhaps Richard Wentworth may be somewhat more cooperative."

CHAPTER 9
SPIDER INSURANCE

THE SOUND of that miniature landslide, which may have been Richard Wentworth's death knell, was still tingling in Jackson's ears as the Hindus rushed him back across the Riverside Drive pathway and into their waiting car. Back downtown it sped. But soon he noticed that it was not heading for the establishment where they had left Swami Rastra. Instead, the driver made for Lexington Avenue and finally turned into a side street in the Twenties, to stop at a building Jackson had never seen before.

Carefully, they guarded him until he was inside and then led him to a narrow, barely furnished bedroom on the third floor. The uninviting cubby-hole was little better than a cell. Even the half-size window was strongly barred with a grille that had been arranged to appear decorative.

"I trust that you will be comfortable here, Mr. Went-worth." The Hindu leader could not keep the smirk out of his dark eyes. "Swami Rastra will see you in the morning."

And before Jackson could remonstrate the door closed and a key turned gratingly in the rusty lock.

The building was ancient and musty smelling, a dilapidated tenement that should have been condemned and torn down. Vermin of all sorts infested it. As Jackson sat on the edge of the cot, disgustedly viewing the dirty, cracked walls, he noticed a spider at work in a web that partially spanned the window opening.

113

Suddenly, the busy little creature gave him the germ of an idea. He stepped up close, caught it as it scurried back to the vortex of its web, and imprisoned it in the hollow top of his fountain-pen.

Breakfast was served to him in his room the next morning. Several hours later his jailer appeared again to announce that Swami Rastra desired his presence below.

The dark-skinned swami awaited him in a room that seemed to be his office. Beturbaned and golden-masked, his Oriental garb seemed strangely out of keeping with the mahogany office desk at which he sat, the stack of morning newspapers spread before him.

"Good morning, Wentworth," he greeted, as if they were old friends. "I see that the police found the body of your impersonator—but they hardly do him justice. Look here." He pointed to a paragraph on one of the inside pages. " 'The body of an unidentified man who had been shot to death and dumped over the Riverside Drive bluff was discovered early this morning near One Hundredth Street'… An unidentified man—that's no way to treat such a clever masquerader!"

"You'd hardly expect the commissioner to announce that the fellow was one of his pet detectives," Jackson grinned. He silently thanked Wentworth for having arranged that notice to help allay any possible suspicions still lingering in the swami's mind.

"I admit that I was not certain last night which of you was the genuine Wentworth," Rastra confessed as he laid the paper aside. "To tell you the truth, I did not greatly care. One of you,

I knew, would be killed before the night was over—the other would still be in my hands. However, I prefer to have Richard Wentworth alive. Now, that there is no longer any doubt of your identity, I am ready to talk business with you."

Calmly, brazenly, he outlined the sordid details of his heinous scheme to clutch New York society by the throat and hold it helpless, while his underlings stripped their writhing victims of their fortunes, their honor, even their lives. Craftily, he pointed out ways in which Wentworth's cooperation would expedite their work and make the ghoulish pickings easier, greater.

As he listened, Jackson managed to unscrew the top of his fountain-pen, tap it on the desk-top as he pretended to drum his fingers thoughtfully. When he leaned back in his chair, the liberated spider scurried across the papers.

Swami Rastra caught a glimpse of that furry little body and leaped back as if shot.

"That thing—that spider—it's an omen," he muttered uneasily, Then he got hold of himself, eyed Jackson steadily. "The Spider is the real reason why you are here," he admitted. "I have heard a great deal about that gentleman, and have a very genuine respect for him. From the start of my operations, I feared that sooner or later the Spider would attempt to interfere. I knew, however, that the Spider has worked on the same side of several cases as Richard Wentworth. It is rumored that he is a friend of Wentworth's."

He explained. "For that reason, I tried to have you eliminated the moment you were brought into my affairs by Stuart Johnson and the Crosbys. When you evaded my best efforts to have you killed, or framed—and when you refused to be warned off—I decided that the next best thing would be to work with you so that the Spider would keep his hands off. I am glad now that our efforts to eliminate you did not succeed—for the Spider has made the appearance I expected. Last night he raided one of my places and killed half a dozen of my men. That was before he understood that Richard Wentworth is now my partner!"

So that was the reason he was still alive—the reason he and Wentworth were not both quietly murdered the night before. He was being held as insurance against the Spider! Jackson had no misconception of what that meant. He was to all intents a prisoner, his life depending on the assistance he gave Swami Rastra and his devilish Hindus….

JACKSON HAD no course but to comply—to hope and watch for a chance to get the upper hand and make his escape or get in touch with Wentworth. His orders had been to carry out the impersonation until he was rescued. How far Wentworth would expect him to go was a question which vexed him sorely during the next three days.

Swami Rastra expected results from his new ally. His sharp eyes were constantly alert to detect the slightest sign of vacillation, or evidence that this Richard Wentworth was attempting to betray him. To carry off his role, Jackson was forced to take part in several crimes that made his fingers itch to turn on his dark-skinned companions and throttle them.

Two wealthy homes he was forced to help loot. He made a careful notation of the exact amount of the thievery, so that full restitution might later be made. Twice he had to lure Wentworth's socialite friends into blackmail situations—hoping fervently that he would have an opportunity to put them in possession of a tip that would reach Wentworth or the police.

But the wily Orientals were too vigilant. Once the victims were contacted, he was given no opportunity to speak to them, no opportunity even to be seen by them. He was simply the bait—and once the bait had been nibbled it was put back.

Finally, on the third day, he could stand it no longer. That noon when his jailer brought his meal, Jackson seemed to be sleeping. But the moment the fellow's back was turned, the sleeper leaped upon him. Grabbing the Hindu's throat, Jackson choked back his yell of surprise and beat him into insensibility.

Lowering the fellow to the verminous cot, he ran exploring fingers through his clothes, frisked him for a weapon. He found only a knife. Armed with that, he stepped out into the corridor and stole stealthily to the head of the stairs. The house seemed to be quiet—so quiet that the old stairway creaked loudly each time he lowered himself another step.

But nobody seemed to hear. The second floor hallway was clear, which left only one more flight. Cautiously, Jackson started down. Then suddenly the uncarpeted steps flattened out beneath him, became a slippery toboggan that whipped his feet out from under and sent him sliding spread-eagled to the bottom—where half a dozen Hindus were waiting.

Before he could get to his feet, they had overwhelmed him, dragging him back up the reconstructed stairs, to throw him into his cell and lock the door.

It was after midnight before anyone came near him again.

Then it was Swami Rastra who was his visitor. The swami stood in the doorway and smiled broadly, mask-rimmed eyes alight with evil satisfaction.

"I have news which should interest you, Mr. Wentworth," he purred. "It should make you a little more anxious to work with us."

From his pocket, he had taken a sheet of paper which he unfolded and began to read. It was a confession from some girl who had swindled her friends out of a fortune, then gone on to other crimes to cover herself.

"The young lady who dictated that is Miss Nita van Sloan!" Rastra finished triumphantly. "She is now a 'guest' in one of my sanctuaries—where her comfort and safety will depend entirely upon you." Abruptly, the grin vanished from his face, and his voice became hard, steel-edged. "You don't want the revelations in that document to become public property, Wentworth," he snapped. "You don't want what this foolish girl has done revealed to the friends she victimized—or to the police. It's up to you whether they remain secret or are broadcast to the world. I have had enough of your stalling. Either you will come in with us whole-heartedly, or a copy of this statement goes, first of all, to your good friend, the police commissioner!"

Jackson's eyes narrowed, as he listened to that ultimatum. His brain churned feverishly.

The confession, he knew, was false. Either it had been invented by Rastra or concocted by Nita in an attempt to gain the attention of the Hindus—perhaps in the hope of being able to locate him. Whether or not she was a prisoner was doubtful. That also might be a deliberate lie to force his hand.

But Swami Rastra seemed to read his mind. The crafty smile came back onto the half-masked face, and he held out his open hand. In the palm lay a ring Jackson would have recognized anywhere—a diamond solitaire that Wentworth had given Nita and which she never removed from her finger.

"I see you recognize this," Rastra taunted. "Perhaps now you will realize that I mean exactly what I say."

Now Jackson knew that there was no longer room for doubt. Nita, like himself, had fallen into the Hindus' hands. Now her safety, as well as his own, depended upon his compliance with the swami's wishes. But with Wentworth seeking both of them, speedy discovery and liberation was doubly assured.

"You win, Rastra," he shrugged resignedly. "What have you got up your sleeve?"

"That's better—much better," Swami Rastra grinned widely. He proceeded to outline a crime that sent cold chills up and down Jackson's spine—a daring crime that would brand Richard Wentworth as a thief who was preying on his friends!

But Jackson must pretend to go through with it—would have to take a part until he could thwart it, even though his rebellion meant death for himself and Nita van Sloan!

CHAPTER 10
RICHARD WENTWORTH—
THIEF

IF RICHARD WENTWORTH had had any hope that the destruction of Gooja Singh's establishment, and the man's death, would check the wave of crime that now terrorized New York society, events of the next few days put an end to it. With Nita's help he had contacted as many of the women he had heard mentioned in the Hindus' conference as he could remember. He had warned them not to be lured into the hands of any soothsayer, and asked that they pay a dummy visit to Ram Singh.

This many, at least, he was able to snatch out of the encircling grip of the blackmail ring.

But despite this interference, the steadily mounting role of crimes seemed to go on without interruption. Robberies, defalcations, swindles, suicides and disappearances—one followed the other. Always the victims were wealthy society people, and the guilty parties, where apprehended, were men and women who moved in the same exclusive social circles. Police activity seemed to be at a stand-still, and although Stanley Kirkpatrick hammered away at his theory that rich idlers were at the bottom of the trouble, his men had been unable to substantiate it. No one could penetrate that cloak of silence which stubbornly sealed the lips of everyone of these confessed society criminals they managed to jail.

After the fiasco of the raid on the empty house, Kirkpatrick had paid no more attention to Wentworth's Hindu theory.

Now Wentworth had no desire to bring it up again for fear the police might institute a Hindu clean-up that could only result in Jackson's death.

To locate Jackson was his own job, and he intended to do it—even though he now seemed to be making scant headway.

Ram Singh, Wentworth believed, offered the best possibility of contacting Swami Rastra's blackmail ring. But waiting for the Hindus to nibble at that bait meant a matter of days, perhaps even weeks—a tantalizing period of inaction when what he wanted was swift action. By the third day, Ram Singh had been contacted by the swami's men. But he dared not seem anxious, too willing. To give in too readily might make them suspicious and ruin the whole plan.

That night the morning newspapers came out with Mayor Wallace's threat to close up every nightclub in town unless the wave of lawlessness abated. During the afternoon, Kirkpatrick had called another meeting of the proprietors and had listened to John Petrillo, their chairman, make an impassioned plea for leniency and fair play.

"We are doing everything in our power to keep our places free of undesirables," he argued. "We have hired extra guards— ex-policemen—whose duty it is to turn away all known Underworld characters and keep a sharp watch over our guests. We are anxious to cooperate with the police, in every way. But it isn't fair to hold us responsible because someone, who happens to be in one of our places, is robbed after he leaves. That is no more reasonable than to close up the theater he might have attended earlier in the evening."

But the police commissioner turned a deaf ear, and Mayor Wallace stood solidly behind him.

From his hotel room Wentworth telephoned Nita and found that she was not at home. He learned from the doorman that she had left an hour previously with another young lady. That was strange—she had intended to stay at home that night and had mentioned nothing about an engagement.

Vaguely uneasy, he called again an hour or two later, and again after midnight—but still she had not returned. Nor was she at home the next morning. Wentworth's message, asking her to call him, was still waiting in her box.

Now thoroughly alarmed, he started his search. But it seemed that nobody had seen her since she walked out of the Riverside Towers with her unknown companion. Sutton Place, Ram Singh, her intimate friends—one after the other, these leads proved fruitless.

That conversation with Ram Singh had seemed strange, Wentworth mused as he put the receiver back onto its hook. The Sikh had been oddly distant, almost uncommunicative—as if someone were there with him, and he could not talk. Probably a client, Wentworth decided, and forgot the matter in his anxiety over Nita.

There was no clue, until he chanced a far-fetched call at the

· JACKSON ·

· NITA VAN SLOAN ·

Crosby home. Then he learned that Anice Crosby, too, had disappeared the night before and not been heard from since!

Preston Kendall, Wesley Brewster, and now Anice Crosby and Nita—that growing list of mysterious disappearances was baffling. But Wentworth reminded himself that these were only a few of the score or more who had dropped out of sight in the city during the past month. Kidnapings or suicides had been the generally accepted verdict in those cases—all part of this baffling crime wave which seemed to have no answer.

The reign of lawlessness must already have piled up millions of dollars for the merciless devil who was behind it, he calculated. But there seemed to be more than money at stake. Many of these crimes had been utterly ruthless, needlessly vicious, beyond any hope of mere gain. It was almost as if this Swami Rastra, whoever he might be, was deliberately warring on New York's high society, striking down one of its members after the other.

And now Nita appeared to be listed among his victims!

Was this because the swami had uncovered Jackson's masquerade? Was Nita's kidnaping the fellow's answer—his retaliation? But, if so, why had Anice Crosby disappeared as well? What could the swami want with her, now that her family was ruined, almost destitute? She was useless to him—unless she had been the bait that had lured Nita into his trap!

Questions… maddening questions that he could not answer, as he paced back and forth in the hotel room that had become like a prison cell to him. Nita was in danger, needed him. He could sense that, knew it as surely as if she was whispering it into his ear. And there was nothing he could do to help her!

Nita was gone—*gone!* That thought hammered through his brain, endlessly.

Absently, his eyes happened to rest on a calendar that hung on the wall. He noticed the date, December fourth. The black numeral seemed to taunt him. December the fourth was the date of the ultra-fashionable winter fashion show and dance at the Ambassador. It was the outstanding social event of the pre-holiday season that Nita had been planning so eagerly to attend.

Tonight he was to have taken her there....

JACKSON STARED at himself in the cracked mirror in his cell-room, and groaned inwardly. Nita had done her work well; too well. The semi-permanent make-up she had applied to his face was as good as when she had put it on. Since then he had touched it up a bit, but that was hardly necessary; his disguise was still only too convincing.

Now, in these evening clothes, he knew that he would be taken for Richard Wentworth by anyone who did not get too close a look at his face—which was exactly what Swami Rastra wanted. It was part of his devilish plan that Richard Wentworth should be very much in evidence tonight, mingle with the people who knew him, and use his identity to direct a crime that would leave the city stunned.

Carefully, Rastra had explained every detail of that plan, explained just the part he was to have in it. Jackson had had no choice but to agree and feign enthusiasm. If he failed, he knew that Nita van Sloan's life would be forfeited—and with her death on his head he would never again be able to face the Major....

When a key turned in the lock of his door, Jackson realized that the time to start had arrived. Downstairs on the first floor the queer company that were to be his companions assembled under Swami Rastra's critical eyes. A Hindu rajah, four fairly light-skinned waiters, an eight-piece orchestra, two dancers—and Richard Wentworth!

125

The gold-masked swami nodded his head in approval, and the bejeweled rajah led the way to four cars that waited at the curb. They headed uptown and finally drew up at different entrances of the Ambassador Hotel. Jackson and the rajah were delivered beneath the canopy in the front, the waiters taken to the employees' door. The rest of the party went through a side entrance that was designated for entertainers.

All converged on the main ballroom where the Ambassador's winter fashion show was in progress.

With the stately rajah close at his side, Jackson strode through the brilliant assemblage and made for a spot in the balcony from which he could command a view of the entire hall. It was crowded with the elite of the city—men dominant in finance and industry, lovely women clad in expensive gowns and bedecked with some of the most famous jewels in the world. It was a king's ransom down there on that polished floor—a haul such as no pirate ever had dreamed of.

And at that very moment dark, avaricious eyes were feasting upon it!

Jackson glanced at his watch. It was almost time. Now the master of ceremonies had stepped out on the low platform at the farther end of the room, holding up his hand for quiet.

"A special feature of this evening's entertainment will be a demonstration of the rhumba as it is performed in Cuba," he announced. "We have been fortunate in securing the services of one of the most accomplished dancing teams, who have brought with them their own orchestra from their native island. Ladies and gentlemen, I give you—Juan and Juanita!"

Applause….

In the hush that followed, the lights blinked out and a lone spot painted a white pool in the center of the floor. Out of the darkness came the low, plunking chords of a guitar, and into the cone of brilliant light floated the dark-skinned, flashing-eyed dancers. For a moment, they postured there in each other's arms.

"Now!" the rajah's voice commanded at Jackson's ear—and the fellow's hand whipped up an automatic, brought it down over the head of the man who was operating the lights.

Tight-lipped, Jackson stepped into the fallen man's place and took hold of the spotlight. He shifted it so that it came to rest on two masked, dark-skinned figures who stood at one side of the room holding open a big burlap bag. They were two of the "specially imported" musicians. The other six, Jackson knew, were by now posted at half a dozen vantage points from which they could cover the hall with the sub-machine-guns they had carried in their innocent-appearing instrument cases.

"Dim the lights!" the voice at his side commanded savagely. Jackson reached for the controls, snapping on the weak emergency lights that cast a pale glow over the hall.

Even that inadequate lighting was sufficient to reveal the masked men crouched over their tommy-guns, the menacing figures that blocked each of the exits. After the first momentary shock of surprise, the crowded hall began to hum with excitement. Women shrilled frantic questions, screamed in abject terror when they received no answers. Men started to surge forward, angrily demanding an explanation—only to see those dark trigger-fingers tensing, tightening ominously on the trips that would release the scything death from the unwavering gun muzzles.

"Stand where you are!" the voice of the rajah commanded brittlely. "Nobody will get hurt, unless you make it necessary. But if anyone is foolish enough to attempt resistance the responsibility for what happens is your own. Line up! Single file! Over there at the right side of the room!" his orders lashed at them. "Go slowly past those men with the bag. Remember, machine-guns are watching your every movement. *Move!*"

A MAN Jackson recognized as the president of the Consumers' National Bank took the lead. Stiffly, he approached the waiting Hindus, face grim, hands held over his head. Swiftly probing hands lifted his wallet, stripped a ring off his finger. Then he was ordered on, as the thieves turned to the trembling woman who came next, and relieved her of her jewels.

Now the line was forming, lengthening, as the victims finally understood what was demanded. Desperately, some tried to hide their more valuable possessions. But the eyes of the watchful rajah seemed to miss nothing.

"It is useless to try to hide your jewelry!" his voice whipped out a warning. "Every move you make is being watched. Every jewel will be found, if we have to strip the lot of you to do it. You, there at the head of the line—where is that necklace you were wearing? Rip off her dress—she has it on her!"

Before the woman could move, they had hold of her. The evening gown was torn in shreds from her scantily clothed body. They snatched the string of priceless matched pearls she had slipped into her bosom. Sobbing hysterically, the woman was led away by her friends… and the line snaked forward while the fortune in that open sack mounted rapidly.

A few of those erstwhile merrymakers still thought that the whole thing was a joke—a special act put on for their entertainment. They jested, as they dropped their valuables into the bag, warned the masked men to be careful of them. An elderly matron, reaching the head of the line, laughingly snatched at one of the masks.

Instantly, the automatic in the rajah's hand roared. The woman screamed once—then sprawled horribly on the floor, while the shuddering line passed her with fearfully averted eyes.

Every moment since he had stepped into that room, Jackson had been sternly holding himself in check. His every inclination was to tear the weapon from the rajah's hand, turn it against him and lead the bolder spirits in that assemblage in a revolt that would overwhelm the thieves. But it would mean bloodshed, a ghastly slaughter. Even if it succeeded, the Hindus who were killed or captured would be only pawns in the game. Swami Rastra would still be at large, free to turn vengeance against Nita van Sloan….

When that woman was shot down cold-bloodedly, all reason left Jackson. Fiercely, he whirled on the rajah—only to find the automatic pressed against his breastbone. Strong arms seized him from behind, as one of the pseudo-waiters yanked him back, held him powerless.

"Back!" the rajah snarled savagely. "One more move like that, and I will order those guns loosed on your friends downstairs. You will be blamed for it, Mr. Wentworth!"

As he spoke, he seized the spotlight—and suddenly it played full on Jackson's features. Pilloried up there on the balcony, he was starkly revealed to the whole assemblage so that recognition was inevitable.

"Richard Wentworth!" a man's voice gasped in shocked amazement—and Jackson's very soul seemed to shrivel and die within him.

Then the spotlight was back on the head of the line of victims. But the damage had been done. Richard Wentworth was branded as a thief. Hundreds of his friends would swear that they had seen him directing that raid—that the bullet which added murder to the crime of robbery had come from the balcony where he stood!

Sick with despair, the realization that he had failed miserably, Jackson watched the hold-up with haggard, bleak-staring eyes. He tensed himself for a desperate leap over the balcony railing; a wild charge into those guns that would at least bring him death. With death would come the recognition that would clear Wentworth of those atrocious charges.

Jackson tensed… and then stared, wide-eyed.

The rhumba dancers had disappeared, when the spotlight was shifted from them. But now they had returned, were whirling into cleared space in the center of the floor. But they were *different!* The girl was the same, but her partner—was the somber-clad Spider!

For a moment they pirouetted there, almost touching that miserable line-up. A weird, cackling laugh, that sounded like the scream of a mad thing, echoed through the big room. Then, suddenly the girl was flung to one side, and her partner made a dive for the masked men at the head of the hold-up line.

After that first instant of stunned surprise, bullets sought him vengefully. Tommy-guns chattered and automatics barked. But by then the Spider was behind those quaking Hindus, holding them in front of him as shields while his blazing automatics sped swift death to wherever a gun muzzle blazed. Instantly, those human shields were riddled. But the Spider seized one of the slumping bodies, held it upright and half over his shoulder, as he charged a doorway and cut down the masquerading waiters who barred the way.

Back into the center of the room he danced, now protected only by his flowing cloak and the agility with which he managed to be in half a dozen spots at once. One by one, those tommy-guns were stilled, the killers behind them either slumped on the floor or fleeing in mad panic.

Bitterly, the rajah cursed. He held his fire, waited murderous-eyed until his aim was sure. At that moment, Jackson broke loose from the fellow who still clung to him. He sprang upon the faker, smashed the gun out of his hand, and leaped over the balcony railing to the floor below.

Through the wild press of screaming men and women, he fought his way toward that raven-hued avenger—but just as he was within sight of the Spider something crashed down on his head with stunning, blinding force. Dazed, only half-conscious, Jackson felt himself falling. Hands dragged him back, as he struggled frantically to break loose and shout vainly for help....

CHAPTER 11
THE DEVIL SETS THE STAGE

I T TOOK Ram Singh less than twenty-four hours, after he returned from his interview with Swami Rastra, to realize his helplessness. His new servants were, in reality, his jailers. They made no attempt to conceal their true mission. One of them was with him always, the others close within call. Next day, he was not permitted out of their sight. Even when reading his crystal for a client, he knew that sharp eyes were watching him, alert ears listening from behind the draperies.

When his telephone rang, one of them was beside him to hear every word of the conversation. When he tried to send a telegram, a censor was at his elbow—the messenger seized at the door, and relieved of the note Ram Singh had managed to slip into his palm. It was useless to try to get word to anyone on the outside, equally useless to attempt escape. Twice he almost reached the door—only to find one of the servants in his path, and to feel a gun muzzle pressed into his back.

They seemed to be everywhere. Yet Ram Singh's eyes were as alert and watchful as theirs. Patiently, he waited until his opportunity came. The doorman was at his post, one of his mates preparing food in the kitchen. The other was here alone.

Suddenly Ram Singh was at the fellow's side, a sharp-pointed knife pricking into the hollow of his throat—jabbing deeper as he tried to scream.

"Another sound, and it drives through to your spine!" Ram Singh hissed a warning.

Quickly, Ram Singh gagged and bound him, stowing him away in a dark corner. He was ready when the food-bearer arrived from the kitchen. The moment he set down his tray, Ram Singh's knife was at his throat, threatening to slit it from ear to ear. Helplessly, the fellow stood there while he was trussed up like his mate. Now remained only the man at the door.

Ram Singh started toward him. But the Hindu must have read his danger in the Sikh's lithe stride, the grim lines of his stern face. Frantically, he grabbed for his automatic, got it from its holster—then dropped it from convulsed fingers, as a gleaming blade streaked across the hallway and plunged through his eye into the brain.

Leaving one of the trussed-up servants where he lay, Ram Singh hauled the other out into the hallway where he could see that ghastly-faced corpse. Plucking the slim-bladed knife from its eye-socket sheath, he turned back to his captive. The Hindu was trembling with fear. Frenziedly, he tried to wriggle away from that bloody point now hovering threateningly over his face.

"His fate will be yours, worthless dog," Ram Singh promised grimly, "unless you have the wisdom to take me to the headquarters of the foul creature you call your master. We are going to the house of him who calls himself the Swami Rastra."

The bound man nodded, endeavoring to speak from behind the gag. Docilely, he agreed the moment his lips were free, swore by all his gods that he would attempt no treachery.

Ram Singh gave him little chance for that. The knife was ready at his fingertips, as they drove downtown in a taxicab— was at the fellow's back when he rang the bell at a doorway on

Half a dozen men and women sat on the floor, their

horrified eyes trained on the suffering girl.

East Twenty-sixth Street. The moment that door opened, Ram Singh hurled him out of the way and charged into the hallway, to slit the doorman's arm from wrist to elbow as he tried to draw a weapon.

Three more Hindus came running at the fellow's scream. Ram Singh welcomed them with an icy smile. Before they could touch him, his knife had disemboweled one, driven deep into the breast of another—and sunk, quivering, between the shoulders of the third as he tried to dash to cover.

That seemed to be all of them. Now there remained only to locate the swami. Ram Singh strode over the body of the man who had tried to flee, went down the hall toward the door. It opened onto a room that was in darkness. Ram Singh stepped inside, felt along the wall for a switch—and the door clicked shut behind him.

Before he could locate that switch, he noticed that the air was becoming strangely heavy. It choked him—the room was being flooded with gas!

The door behind him had locked, would not open when he tugged at it. But now his eyes were becoming accustomed to the darkness. He could make out another door at the other end of the room. Groggily, he staggered to it, yanked it open and staggered out into a narrow corridor—that now suddenly gave way beneath him.

Out from under his feet went the floor. But at the same moment a rope dropped over his head, slipped down over his body, fastened around his ankles. In the next moment, he pitched wildly in midair, stopped short with a jerk—and hung helplessly by his feet.

Lights flashed on around him, and two Hindus warily approached to secure his arms. They tied him up so that he could barely move a muscle. He could merely hang there and look into the grinning face of the masked swami who gloated over his discomfiture.

"Your arrival is most opportune, Kira Singh," Swami Rastra mocked. "You are such an excellent actor that I shall have a star role for you to play before morning!"

IT WAS while he had stopped at the Crosby home, in the course of his search for Nita, that Wentworth had first been impressed by the peculiarly virulent quality of that strange criminal war on New York's society. While talking with Elizabeth Crosby, Anice's bereaved mother, he had realized how severe was the suffering of this particular family.

The father and son were dead, disgraced, the daughter had mysteriously disappeared—and yet even this did not seem to be the end.

"It seems that an evil fate is hanging over all of us," the poor woman had bemoaned. "Mr. Crosby, Allen—and now Anice. Even my older daughter, Margaret, is suffering from it. She will not admit it to me, but I can see that she is in mortal fear of something that she is desperately keeping to herself. I have read the terror in her eyes. I can see how worry is affecting her."

Mrs. Crosby, a proud descendant of one of New York's oldest and finest families, was herself a broken woman.

Only bitter vindictiveness could account for such relentless hounding of broken and impoverished victims—only a deep hatred of high society itself. So Wentworth mused as he paced his hotel room. Such hatred would account for much that had transpired—the dishonor besmirching many a highly respected name, the ruination that had come upon some of the city's proudest families, the barbarity of that wanton slaughter in front of St. Bartholomew's on Thanksgiving morning. It might as well show its hand again at the most exclusive function of the social season, the Ambassador dance that night....

It was for that reason that Wentworth had disguised himself so that none of his friends would recognize him, and attended the occasion, even though he could not take Nita as planned.

The moment he had seen a man, who appeared to be himself, walk into the room, he knew that something was about to happen. One glance at Jackson's cleverly made-up face had told him that the chauffeur was there under compulsion—and from that moment he was alert for the first sign of trouble.

As soon as the lights went out for the feature rhumba, Wentworth glimpsed shadowy shapes darting from the musician's platform. In the same moment, he had run to a screen at one corner of the room and, with lightning fingers, donned the Spider's make-up. When he came scuttling from cover, the hold-up was in full progress—high time for the Spider to take a hand!

Men had gone down all around him in the mad mêlée that followed—some to crawl to cover, as the guns roared over their heads, others to lie there oblivious to the bedlam raging around them. Men whom he knew, with whom he often had dined.

Then, right ahead of him in the thick of the crowd, he saw Jackson desperately pushing his way through—only to go down as three masked men seized him.

Wentworth tried to get his guns clear and cut down those dark-skinned snatchers. But at that moment half a dozen hysterical, shrieking women ran in front of him. Before he could fight clear, Jackson was gone—dragged through a doorway at the far end of the room.

That doorway led into a short corridor where the service elevators were located. Wentworth plunged through it. He was just in time to see Jackson being shoved into one of the cars. The Hindus leapt in after him, as the door clanged shut. No time now to wait for another elevator; it was quicker to use the stairs.

Half a dozen steps at a time, Wentworth sped from landing to landing. But when he reached the ground floor, and ran out onto the delivery platform, it was deserted. There was nothing in the narrow alleyway but a small-sized delivery van just swinging out into the street. Wentworth raced after it, reached the street. He darted across the way, leaped into a taxi and jammed an automatic into the face of the gaping driver.

"That van!" he ordered. "Follow it—and don't let it get away from you!"

The driver's mouth dropped open and his eyes bulged, but he stepped on the gas. Doggedly, he clung to the tail-lights that were now nearly a block away, crept up on them as they sped down Lexington Avenue, and had nearly overhauled them when the van swung into East Twenty-seventh Street. It came to a halt in front of a building a third of a way down the block.

"This will do," Wentworth called, and flipped a bill into the cabby's lap, as the fellow sat there, saucer-eyed.

From a doorway near the corner, Wentworth watched. Several people were led from the van into the hallway of a shabby-looking tenement. Then, the truck again got under way. Wentworth scurried to the doorway of the building, past the unlocked door and into the grimy hallway. It was utterly still, but his keen ears caught a muffled sound from the rear. He sprinted down the long corridor and yanked open a door leading to the back yard.

At the rear of that yard was a fence that was now behaving very peculiarly, indeed. A section of it was swinging shut, like a revolving door. But before it could close completely, he had dived through the opening into the yard beyond. This yard was in the rear of what appeared to be a warehouse. It was small, less than ten feet deep—and the only way out of it was by means of a basement door into the building.

Wentworth tried the door, found that it opened, and stepped into a stygian corridor beyond. Picking his way warily with his pencil-flash, he prowled through the dusty, junk-littered rooms. There was nobody there, and he was at the foot of the stairs, about to try the floor above, when he caught the faint sound of a shrill scream.

The scream came from *below!*

Carefully, he went over the basement again, until he found what seemed to be a closet. Actually, it was a stairway leading down into a pit of blackness—deep down to a sub-cellar, cold and damp. A veritable medieval dungeon, undoubtedly designed for the storage of stolen goods when the building evidently had served as a fence for thieves.

Wentworth paused at the foot of the steps. The terrified scream rang out again. After it came the voice of a woman, fervently pleading… and ending in a shriek of agony!

Quickly, he located the source of that sound—a chamber toward the front of the building. Light shone through the partially closed doorway. Gun in hand, he padded toward it— and found himself staring into a grotto rigged up like a Hindu temple. It was a large room, with a throne-like arrangement mounted on a dais at one end. On that throne sat the richly robed figure of Swami Rastra, his golden half-mask in place beneath the folds of an elaborate turban!

IN THE center of the chamber was a ten-foot metal image of the goddess Kali, a savage-looking creature with jagged, bloody teeth protruding from her gaping mouth, a huge serpent twined around her waist. She gripped a club, and one of her feet was pressed down on a squirming body. That figure underfoot should have been an image of Siva, her husband, Wentworth knew. Instead, it was the body of a young woman who was pinned flat beneath the metal limb!

Helpless under the threatening knives of savage-looking, half-naked Hindu guards, half a dozen men and women, well known in New York society, squatted on the stone floor around the image. Their horrified eyes stared at the suffering girl and the cruel-faced Oriental who stood beside the hideous goddess, grasping a lever attached to the statue's base.

"So you thought you could defy Swami Rastra, did you?" a

taunting voice mocked them from the dais. "Watch, and you will learn the price of disobedience. Now, Pertab!"

The man at the lever grinned with evil anticipation. His arm drew back—and the belly of the image slid open! Where there had appeared to be nothing but solid metal, a hole nearly two feet square now gaped—and out of it poured a dozen deadly snakes hissing angrily as they cascaded down on the screaming victim!

That much Wentworth saw—and then the Spider was charging into that hellish den. Through the doorway he leaped, guns ready. But the moment he was inside, the floor seemed to tremble, quake, beneath his feet. Was it a trapdoor? Apprehensively, he glanced down. But it was from overhead that the menace came.

Barely in time, he leaped back out of the way—as a huge python dropped from an opening in the ceiling and fell directly in his path!

Wentworth's guns battered the weaving head of the creature, poured bullets into those thick, writhing coils, as he danced out of reach of their crushing embrace. Now pandemonium was raging in that subterranean chamber. The screams of the terrified prisoners were mingling with the shrieks of Kali's helpless, fear-crazed captive. And above the uproar another voice was shouting lustily.

Out from the darkness at one side of the chamber had rushed a new figure—the figure of Richard Wentworth himself!

"Look out!" the disguised Jackson yelled. "This is a trap!"

But Wentworth had reached the side of the image, and was

making a desperate effort to save the life of the terrified girl. Firing carefully, so as not to hit her flailing arms and legs, he made every bullet count as he shot the heads off some of those poisonous serpents, then pounded the rest with the empty guns when his clips were exhausted.

To his surprise, none of the Hindus attacked him while he was occupied with that perilous task. But when he whirled to confront them, he found the answer to his strange immunity—the Orientals had disappeared. All except Swami Rastra, who still sat there on the dais.

Clubbed automatic held ready for the first treacherous move, Wentworth leaped toward him. A mocking laugh rang in his ears. Springing up to that devilish throne, he grasped the edge of the metal mask and tore it away—to reveal the clean shaven face of Ram Singh!

The Sikh had been drugged, could only sit there and mutely voice his misery with anguished eyes!

Again that taunting laugh echoed through the chamber, but now Wentworth knew that it came from the far, dark corner of the room through which he had entered.

"The Spider, Richard Wentworth, and faithful old Ram Singh—now you are all together!" Swami Rastra's voice jeered. "I regret that I cannot stay and join your party. But be assured that you are getting off very easily. You will not experience half the unpleasantness that awaits Nita van Sloan and Anice Crosby tomorrow noon. That, I promise you, will be an occasion that will make social history in this fine city!"

WENTWORTH WAS leaping toward the sound of that

taunting voice, before it finished. But when he reached the end of the room, the heavy metal door through which he had come clanged shut in his face. A heavy bolt rasped solidly into place, then another. He knew that hope of escape in that direction was ended. They were trapped, buried alive down there in that dank tomb fifty feet below the level of the streets!

Obviously, this place was not Swami Rastra's headquarters—the hideout where he was holding Nita and Anice Crosby. This was merely an auxiliary establishment for which he had no more use—a building which he would burn down over their heads—or utilize as a means of turning his trapped enemies over to the police.

The police… that was the answer to this devilish set-up!

Those half-frantic victims who had now leaped up from the floor would swear that the voice they had heard issuing orders had come from the lips of Ram Singh—just as the hundreds of witnesses of the Ambassador hold-up would swear that Richard Wentworth had directed that raid. Wentworth and Ram Singh both were damningly framed. And now the Spider faced unmasking and arrest, if the police raided that sub-cellar….

As those thoughts rushed through Wentworth's mind, he was busy at the side of Kali's statue. He found the lever that liberated the girl imprisoned beneath the metal foot. The moment he had lifted her clear, he started a systematic search for a way out of that dungeon. Carefully, he made a circuit of the damp stone walls, scrutinized every foot carefully with his flashlight. But there was no way of escape. The place had only one door, and that was solidly barred.

And at that moment he caught the sound of police whistles coming faintly from the distance.

Those sounds spelled miraculous deliverance to the wild-eyed captives. Frenziedly, they rushed to the barred door and pounded upon it while they shouted to make sure that their rescuers did not turn back. Reassuring voices were shouting back from the stairway.

And Wentworth took the only alternative left to him. Grasping the side lever, he opened the belly of the image and climbed inside. He reached out to start the lever back into place, and the metal door slid shut—entombing him in Kali's belly!

CHAPTER 12
DEATH'S HIDE-AND-SEEK

CROUCHED LOW in the interior of that grotesque image, Wentworth heard the heavy cellar door creak open. Then the police came swarming into the place and seized Ram Singh. Jackson tried desperately to make them understand the truth, but the liberated prisoners shouted him down. Then a gruff voice cut him short.

"That feller's Wentworth!" a detective identified him, and Jackson made no attempt at dispute. "Yeah, we know all about that—you can save it for the commissioner." The fellow sneered. "Now,—where's this Spider? He's down here somewhere."

Wentworth could hear them ransacking the sub-cellar, their night-sticks tapping on the walls as they sought another door.

Tensely, he waited, expecting every moment that his hiding place would be discovered.

Now one of the men was standing right in front of the image, tugging at the lever, curiously. Noiselessly, the door slid open. But at that moment one of his companions walked over and interfered.

"Better shut that damn thing up," he warned. "There might be more snakes in it—an' I've got no use for them damn things."

Again the panel clicked shut, and Wentworth relaxed, breathed a sigh of relief. Patiently, he crouched there. He heard them decide that the Spider must have had another way out of the place, even though they could not find it. Then he heard them leaving, their footsteps clumping up the steps, fading in the distance. Cautiously, he ran his fingers over the inside of the door, pressed upon it and felt for some sort of hold that would enable him to pull it aside. There was nothing. The panel fitted perfectly, and he was trapped helplessly here—perhaps to be left to starve to death in this metal trap!

Frantically, he put his weight against the door, used all his strength in an attempt to force it. He tried desperately to rock the image, as he threw himself from side to side against its walls. Then he stopped short, as he caught the sound of footsteps returning on the stairway.

"Humph—nice-lookin' gal to keep company with all night," a policeman grunted disgustedly. He came over to the image, and tapped the metal side with his nightstick.

"Good thing the sarge sent me along to chaperone the two of you," his partner chuckled.

Wentworth realized that a police guard had been stationed in the cellar; now he was doubly imprisoned in Kali's dark interior. The help that he needed to escape from his prison was there within a few feet of him. But he was tantalizingly trapped so that he could not call for that aid without revealing himself as the Spider!

During the long hours that he lay cramped in that narrow cell, he had plenty of time to review the events of the day. Again the spiteful vindictiveness of this master-criminal came home to him, forcefully—especially, the fiendish delight Swami Rastra seemed to take in persecuting the Crosbys. Nita and Anice Crosby had been singled out for some particularly diabolical attention. The hounding of Nita was understandable—but why the Crosby girl? Certainly, there was nothing more to be wrung from her ruined family.

But was there? Gradually, a possible answer to that question began to suggest itself. But to follow that half-formed suspicion any farther would take investigation—and that, for the time being, was out of the question.

LONG HOUR after hour, with not a sound but the intermittent conversation of the posted policemen. A dozen times Wentworth glanced at the luminous dial of his watch, as the night hours passed. Then it was morning. The guard in the sub-cellar changed, and still he was hopelessly trapped. Seven o'clock... eight... nine. At last, there was another interruption: Footsteps on the stairs and voices out there in the cellar.

One of those voices was Stanley Kirkpatrick's!

Curiously, the commissioner inspected the place, then came

up to the image and grasped the lever. Wentworth heard it draw back, the panel slid open almost soundlessly. Tensely, he crouched low, gripping one of his reloaded automatics—and then Kirkpatrick's head was poking in through the opening!

Instantly, the muzzle of Wentworth's gun jammed into Kirkpatrick's face. He seized the front of the commissioner's coat, held it.

"Quiet!" he rasped in a harsh whisper. "This is the Spider! You called me into this case, and I answered. I've been doing my part—now you do yours. If your word is worth anything, you will do as I tell you. Call off your men—order them out of here."

Kirkpatrick hesitated, and the gun prodded him.

"A minute more, and I'll pull the trigger!" Wentworth muttered a warning. "Even that will be too good for a liar whose word isn't worth a damn!"

"Okay," Kirkpatrick capitulated softly. He drew his head out of the trap, backed up against the image and sent his men upstairs on quickly invented errands.

Wentworth kept his automatic pressed against the commissioner's spine, until the police had left. But he knew that the gun was nothing more than a bluff. It was not fear of death that had won Stanley Kirkpatrick's cooperation but the appeal to his sense of fair-play—the reminder of that offer he had made in the presence of Richard Wentworth.

The moment the men were gone, the Spider grasped the sides of the opening and vaulted out of his cramped quarters. Curiously, the commissioner turned to stare at this almost legendary creature who had so long managed to elude him.

"Well, Spider—" he began. But in that moment the twisted figure sprang at him like a suddenly released spring.

Strong arms wrapped around Kirkpatrick, bore him to the floor and turned him over on his stomach before he could recover from his surprise. Then he put up a battle, struggling with all his strength. He was powerless in that unyielding grip. Threats and warnings fumed from his lips, but the Spider paid them no attention. Silently, he stripped off the commissioner's coat, shirt and tie—then manacled his wrists with his own handcuffs. Next came the trousers, and Kirkpatrick's ankles were lashed together with his own belt. A handkerchief wadded and tightly secured between his jaws—and only his furious eyes could voice his seething rage.

Lifting the bound man in his arms, Wentworth thrust him into the belly of the image and pulled the lever that sealed him there. Then quickly he went to work removing his make-up—transforming the Spider into a double of New York's police commissioner.

Safe in his disguise as Stanley Kirkpatrick, he strode out of the cellar and out of the empty warehouse above it.

But that disguise would be effective for only fifteen or twenty minutes—only until Kirkpatrick's men returned to the sub-cellar and heard him struggling inside the image. After that, every cop in town would be on the lookout for the masquerader.

WENTWORTH GLANCED at his watch. Half-past nine. Only two and a half hours until noon, but he had to return to his hotel for a change of clothing. Newsboys were shouting an extra, as he hailed a cab—something about Courtney Arnold, the city comptroller. He picked up a paper and ran his eyes over the headlines, as he sank back onto the seat.

"Comptroller Arnold Commits Suicide!" the black letters shrieked. "Latest Blueblood Crime. City Loss Estimated at Million."

Incredulously, he skimmed through the amazing account. Courtney Arnold, the city's socialite comptroller, a man whose advent into public office had been hailed as a triumph for good government, had taken his own life—just when it was about to be revealed that he had engineered a huge fraud involving the city's finances. Faced with certain exposure, he had put a bullet through his head, and had been found dead in bed early that morning by his butler. Arnold's wife and daughter had disappeared, and the servants had no idea of their whereabouts.

Courtney Arnold was the latest victim of the crime wave! But this time Swami Rastra had surely overreached himself! Tampering with the funds of the city was too brazen....

As soon as Wentworth reached his room, he turned on the radio. In a few minutes, the program was interrupted for the news bulletin he expected.

"Following the discovery of Comptroller Arnold's death, Mayor Wallace immediately ordered License Commissioner Humphries to suspend the license of every night-club in the city until further notice," came the announcement. "This order is a drastic attempt to cope with the crime wave which the police believe has its roots in these resorts. It will go into effect at once, and police will be on hand tonight to enforce it."

Mayor Wallace had carried out his threat. But the comptroller's defalcation and suicide had left him no choice, Wentworth admitted as he worked in front of his make-up mirror. It was almost as if the criminal, who was directing this lawless campaign, was deliberately baiting him into closing up the night spots.

The moment Wentworth had restored his own personality, he set about carrying out the plans he had evolved while penned up in the Kali statue. First he hurried to the reference room of the public library and consulted a copy of the *Social Register*. The members of the Crosby family were the ones who interested him, Gilbert and his wife Elizabeth, Allen, Anice—and especially Margaret.

"Margaret Louise Nugent, nee Crosby," read her entry. "Born, June 4, 1909. Married Peter Rowland, April 20, 1926. Marriage annulled, July 8, 1926. Married Paul Nugent, November 10, 1926—"

Two marriages in little more than six months! Now Wentworth recalled some of the details of that brief first marriage twelve years ago. It had been a social scandal of the day. To check his memory, he telephoned to Harvey van Rensselaer, on the society desk of the *Daily Bulletin*.

"Remember Margaret Crosby's first wedding? Well, I guess I do!" van Rensselaer chuckled. "Peter Rowland, her bridegroom, was the Crosby butler—an Englishman. They eloped one night, and when the family heard about it they promptly turned thumbs down on him. Margaret said she would stick with her man no matter what they did about it. She tried to brazen it out—but you know Elizabeth Crosby. When she gave the word, almost every door was closed to them."

The account continued. "The climax came at a swanky reception given by the Hamilton Taylors. Margaret and her butler-husband were invited, but they were snubbed outrageously when they got there. It was so bad that she finally broke down and fled in tears. After that, she gave up and allowed her family to arrange an annulment. Six months later, she married Paul Nugent. He was the choice of her folks, picked out in a hurry before she had a chance to contract any more misalliances."

Wentworth recalled that night. He had not been at the reception, but he had heard its reverberations and had felt sorry for the harried couple. That reception had been given by Hamilton Taylor—and Hamilton Taylor's family had suffered almost as badly as the Crosbys. Hamilton, himself, was a broken man, a self-confessed murderer on the verge of insanity; his daughter Grace was a suicide—and his daughter Mildred's body had been hacked almost beyond recognition before she was allowed to die....

"Rowland?" van Rensselaer answered Wentworth's question. "He disappeared after that. Supposedly, he went back to England and retired on the settlement he had wrung from the Crosbys. He wasn't a bad sort, though, Dick—don't get him wrong. He was about thirty at that time, good-looking, fairly well educated, a former British soldier who had served in India. He was really a gentleman."

A former British soldier in India! Things were at last beginning to click in Wentworth's mind. He began to understand the terror which Margaret Nugent had been unwilling to confide even to her mother.

But whether or not she would talk to her family, she would talk to him—and that in a hurry.

TWENTY MINUTES later he was at her apartment hotel. At the door, he announced himself as a bellboy. When she answered, and caught sight of him, she was panic-stricken. Frantically, she tried to close the door, but his foot was already thrust through the opening. Quickly, he forced his way in and faced her as she stood, wide-eyed and panting, with her hands against the wall behind her, trembling.

"You're—you're from the police!" she gasped. "I knew you would come, but I didn't expect you so soon! How did you know? There has been nobody else here. I only found his body a few minutes—not even half an hour-ago. Don't look at me like that!" She barely repressed a scream. "I *found* him, I tell you—*I didn't do it!*"

"I am not from the police," Wentworth reassured her gently. "I have come here to try to help you. I was a friend of your father's."

Distrust and suspicion flared wildly in her eyes, but as quickly it vanished. She was just a trembling, terrified woman desperately in need of a confidant. Wentworth took her icy hands into his and warded off the hysteria that threatened to overwhelm her.

"It's Paul—my husband," she gasped out her story. "He is there in his bedroom, dead—murdered! I found him that way

153

when he did not come out to breakfast. No, I haven't notified the police. I didn't want to do that—not until I knew. Oh, I don't know what to do!"

"Not until you knew what?" Wentworth pressed. Then, when she did not answer he supplied the words for her. "Not until you knew who had murdered him? Or, shall we say, not until you knew that somebody you have in mind did *not* murder him?"

"Oh, he couldn't have!" the distraught woman half-sobbed. "He wouldn't do that. He said he would sometimes—but he never meant it. But the police will suspect him. Paul always warned me that in case anything happened to him there would be papers left behind blaming Pres—"

"Blaming whom?" Wentworth urged, when her startled lips closed tightly. "Blaming the man who loves you, and his name is—"

"Preston Kendall," fell almost soundlessly from those white lips. "But he couldn't have done a thing like that! He *couldn't!*"

Preston Kendall! One after the other, the pieces were beginning to fall into place. Wentworth's blood leaped with excitement, as he felt that he was closing in—almost within reach of the master-thief and killer he sought!

"Yes, Preston Kendall is my lover," Margaret Nugent admitted with a pathetic flare of defiance. "He has been for years. I never did love Paul Nugent. He mistreated and robbed me almost from the day we were married. It was only natural that I should fall in love with Preston. But my family would not hear of a divorce. The Crosby women do not divorce their husbands—so

I had to go on with it. Preston knew what I was suffering, and he writhed under it…."

Her voice faded to a scared whisper, but Wentworth took up where she had left off.

"You were desperate for a way out. You didn't know where to turn, so you consulted a mystic—this crystal-gazer, Sutra Nahr," he told her. "You told him your troubles—confessed about Kendall, and asked him to find a way out for you."

Silently, she nodded acknowledgment—and Wentworth knew that he had solved the blackmailers' hold on the Crosby family. It was not Allen who had given them the club to wield over his father's head—it was Margaret. Allen, himself, made a victim, had been dragged into the mess; had been forced into crime in his desperate effort to raise money to help her. It was Margaret, helpless in the hands of the blackmailers—helpless in the hands of the man she had once married and then cast aside when her family and friends would not accept him!

Bit by bit, Wentworth drew her out and established the truth of his reasoning.

She knew who was behind this merciless war on her family, knew how bitterly that person hated them—and that was the reason for her terror.

"You have seen Peter Rowland recently, haven't you?" Wentworth fired his question point-blank.

Margaret Nugent barely nodded. "Yes," she whispered. "He is here in town. He is—"

Suddenly, her eyes rounded fearfully. A scream caught in her throat, as a gleaming Oriental knife streaked past her head and slapped broadside against the wall at her back. Instantly, its clattering fall was echoed by the roar of a gun. Blood gushed from between her fingers, as she clutched wildly at her breast and toppled from the chair!

That knife-throwing was a bungling job, Wentworth knew it as he leaped to one side and dived into the next room, then out onto the penthouse terrace. The man who had made the throw was no Hindu....

The killer was just rounding a corner of the penthouse, as he reached the terrace. Wentworth caught a fleeting glimpse of the dark-skinned face of—*Preston Kendall!* Preston Kendall in his Indian prince make-up! Realizing that he had been recognized, he whirled at the edge of the building and blasted a shot at his pursuer.

Wentworth threw himself flat, as a bullet ricocheted off the brick wall. Crouching low, he zigzagged his way to the corner, rounded it.

But the fleeing killer had had time to dash into the foyer by way of another door—time to leap into the elevator and make his escape!

It was too late....

CHAPTER 13
THE GREEN GODDESS FURY

ONLY ONE car came all the way to the roof, Wentworth saw, looking down. Then he was racing to the floor below—to jab his finger against the elevator button until another car, with an indignant operator, answered the persistent call. Once he understood, the operator plummeted the car to the street floor.

"A brown-skinned fellow? Sure, he was just here," the doorman supplied. "He came running out hollering for a taxi. I heard him tell the driver to take him to the Continental—Continental Theater, it sounded like."

But Wentworth was already signaling another cab and barking the Continental Theater destination at the driver. There was no performance of *The Green Goddess* at that time of the morning—but for some reason its recently missing star had business there at the theater. And that business, Wentworth promised himself, would be very much his, as well.

"There's nobody in there, I tell you—the theater's empty," the watchman insisted, when he pounded on the stage entrance door. But when Wentworth's gun was leveled at his belly he gulped and hurriedly backed out of the way.

Into the dark back-stage regions, Wentworth dashed, to prowl through dark, empty-sounding corridors and up narrow metal stairways that led to the dressing-rooms. There was not a sound but the echo of his own footsteps in this huge, barnlike structure—not a sound until a knife slapped against the wall and clattered down onto the iron stairway!

Wentworth stooped, snatched it up and sheathed it under his trouser leg. Then he gave chase to the dark, shadowy figure he had suddenly glimpsed ahead of him. The fellow was racing toward a dressing room door near the corridor's end. Wentworth was almost upon him—when abruptly he pitched headlong, tripped by a heavy wire that had been stretched across his path.

Ahead, he heard a door slam shut. On his feet again, he reached the door at the end of the corridor. It was marked with a silver star—and Wentworth pounded on it with his fists. There was no response. He drew back across the corridor, hurled himself against it. Three times he charged before the lock snapped and ripped away from the wood.

The door flew inward with a bang, Wentworth catfooting into the dressing-room. His guns covered the gasping figure of Preston Kendall, sprawled limply in a chair against the wall. The actor's face was browned with make-up for his role in *The Green Goddess,* but Wentworth could see the deadly pallor beneath the artificial coloring.

Kendall was dying, writhing in the last agonies of poisoning!

"I know—you think I killed Margaret. But I didn't!" he gasped. Wentworth loosened his collar, tried to make him more comfortable. "I have been a prisoner—for days. My God, I don't know how long—it seemed ages! They kept me in a cellar where it was so dark—I couldn't tell night or day. I know why. It was because—because I tried to protect Margaret and her family—from the gang of devils Peter Rowland set on them." He shuddered.

"That was my fault," he rushed on frantically, as if fearing he would not get the words out before death sealed his lips. "It was because I loved Margaret—because of my liaison with her. That's why Rowland was able to get a strangle-hold on her family. He threatened disgrace—to ruin them all. He forced them into crimes that made his hold on them stronger and stronger."

He was panting. "I tried to stop that before it was too late. I was worried particularly—about young Allen. I was in the Savoy Club, watching him—the night Phil Deming was robbed and killed. I knew that Allen was taking desperate chances—to get money to satisfy Rowland's demands. I was afraid he was—mixed up with thieves. That night I saw him go to a phone booth—just as Deming left the club. I stepped into the booth next to it. I heard him tip off the crooks—about that diamond of Mrs. Deming's—and where they were going. I tried to follow the Demings. But before I could interfere—Gooja Singh grabbed me. His men threw me into a car—and took me to that cellar."

He sobbed on. "Since then, I've been a prisoner—until just a little while ago. Then they shaved me and put on my make-up. After that, Peter Rowland came and made me swallow something—poison it must have been. He mocked me. He told me that Nugent and Margaret were dead—and that both murders would be blamed on me. Then they brought me here. They dropped that gun on the floor beside me, said it was the murder weapon—my own gun…."

His strength was ebbing rapidly. Now his voice was barely more than a gasping whisper, but Wentworth bent close to him.

"This Peter Rowland—you know him, Kendall," he urged. "Who is he? Where can I find him?"

Silence, then—

"He is Pet—" Kendall managed, and then his jaws were locked in a spasm of agony—until death brought him merciful relief….

That was all.

WENTWORTH ROSE from beside the corpse, looked thoughtfully around the little dressing-room. Rowland, Swami Rastra, or whatever his name might be, must be close at hand—Kendall could not have been kept a prisoner here backstage all these days. He must have been brought here a short while ago—maybe only minutes ago. Yet the watchman had been certain that there was nobody in the theater.

There must be others—the one who had hurled that knife, those who had brought Kendall into the building.

Warily, Wentworth searched every bit of that back-stage domain, went through all the dressing-rooms. But there was nobody in any of them—not a sound in the place since Kendall had breathed his last. Recalling that the actor had said he was held captive in a cellar, Wentworth searched the basement, engine-room, storage cellars. All were as deserted as the upper portions of the theater. Yet this must be where Kendall was hidden, or the watchman would have seen him being brought into the building....

Wentworth went over the cellar minutely, scrutinizing every square foot beneath the beams of his pocket-light—until he discovered fresh tracks in the dust that lay thick in an unused storage section. Those tracks oddly led up to a blank stone wall and seemed to disappear.

A trick wall—that was the answer. But the button or lever that operated it was well concealed. Wentworth glanced at his watch. It was almost noon—almost time for that "occasion that will make social history" which Swami Rastra had so tauntingly promised.

Feverishly, Wentworth renewed his search. With his fingertips, he went over every inch of the wall. But it was a quarter of an hour before he located the two stones that had to be pressed simultaneously in order to set the mechanism in motion. Noiselessly, a section of that apparently solid masonry moved backward and left room for him to step through into a dark passageway that went deeper into the earth!

Down two flights of steps and along two narrow, dank-smelling corridors he followed the barely distinguishable tracks. Into the very bowels of the dark, cold earth, he seemed to be boring… and then the silence was broken by a terrified shriek that seemed to come from miles away!

Wentworth quickened his pace, padded to the end of that corridor and into another that met it at right angles. Now there was a faint glimmer of light ahead and the sound of low voices. Those voices seemed to be moaning, begging—fervid pleas that were interspersed with sobs and ghastly, terrified screams.

Again the corridor turned, but now it was sloping up to a doorway not more than twenty feet away. A faint night-light burned above it. Cautiously, he approached it, grasped the metal knob, turned it and slowly drew the door open—to stare into a lighted cavern that looked like some mad artist's conception of Inferno.

That room was nothing more than a large, rock-walled dungeon, but nearly fifty people were crowded into it—the

THE SPIDER

principals and witnesses of what appeared to be some sort of hellish marriage ceremony!

At one end of the torch-lit room was a raised platform where Swami Rastra sat presiding over the proceedings. Just in front of the platform stood a frocked clergyman who cowered in the grasp of two half-naked Hindus with long, gleaming bladed knives thrust through their loincloths. The clergyman's hands trembled so that he could hardly hold the little book from which he was reading the marriage service—for an ashen-faced, scantily-clad girl and a grinning Hindu who knelt before him.

The girl was Vera Stanton, one of the season's most beautiful and socially prominent debutantes. Behind her were seven more of her young friends, each gripped possessively by a smiling, lecherous-eyed Hindu. Eight girls whose outrageous travesties of wedding gowns made a startling revelation of their charms for the eager eyes of their smirking husbands-to-be!

Behind them, on the floor, squatted more than a score of their parents and friends—dignified, well bred men and women who had been trussed up so securely that they could do nothing but sit there and watch with helpless, outraged eyes. Either that or fight vainly against their bonds, like that young fellow who was rolling and squirming on the floor.

At that moment Wentworth got a look at his swollen, blood-smeared face. It was Wesley Brewster! Wesley Brewster nearly mad with desperation because, as soon as this burlesque of a marriage ceremony was finished, Anice Crosby would be the next to take her place in front of the profane altar!

That much Wentworth saw before he glimpsed the hell-inspired background of that infernal ceremony—and felt the blood chill in his veins as cold horror clutched at his heart!

ARRANGED IN a semi-circle around that dungeon room were ten more girls. They stood stiff, erect, arms close to their sides, eyes staring in consummate horror through what appeared to be a covering of cellophane sheathing them from head to foot. These girls were like human candles, the sheathing covering gathered together and twisted into a wick above their heads!

There *had been* ten of those human candles—but now there were only seven. Two still stood erect in their places, but were mere blackened, charred corpses—*candles that had burned out!* The third was just going up in smoke. The flames had already stilled her shrieks and were now licking around her knees.

With an "amen" that was a groan of compassion, the haggard-eyed clergyman finished that mockery of a marriage service. The horrified bride was taken into the arms of her newly made husband—to gasp and fall limp.

"Ecstasy—sheer ecstasy!" Swami Rastra's gloating voice mocked as he watched her faint. "The poor child can't stand such happiness—and little wonder. This splendid marriage is more than she ever dared to hope for—a marriage that will guarantee her place in the sacred listing of the *Social Register!* But we mustn't keep the rest of you anxious brides waiting. You are next, Hazar—step forward with your lady. Ah," he beamed, "it is the lovely Miss Crosby! She has a special friend here to light her way to happiness. The third of your charges from the right, Iman."

Iman grinned evilly. He lighted his long taper, stepped down the line of human candles and halted in front of the designated one. Anice Crosby was forced to her knees beside a villainous-looking Hindu, who had to hold her up to keep her from collapsing. Iman had stopped before the transparent-shrouded figure of Nita van Sloan!

The lighted taper rose to the wick top, as the clergyman began to intone the service. But before the wick above Nita ignited, the fellow shrieked and spun around—to drop in a bullet-riddled heap, as the black-cloaked Spider catapulted through the doorway with a howl of rage that struck terror into those brown-skinned fiends!

CHAPTER 14
EXIT THE SWAMI

THE SPIDER'S blazing guns cut down those leering would-be bridegrooms before they had a chance to skulk for protection behind their despairing victims. His berserk rush carried him from the doorway to the center of the room in half a dozen strides—and death seemed to emanate from him on every side. Swami Rastra's men went down—but the swami had been quick to fling himself from his high chair and take refuge behind it.

"Cut him down! Use your knives! He is only one man!" he shrieked.

Sheer desperation drove them forward, heathen yells on their lips, razor-sharp knives in their hands. Deliberately, mercilessly, the Spider blasted them down. But now they had reached him.

The long knives were seeking him, slicing through his cape until it fluttered in black ribbons.

From one end of that dungeon to the other, he fought his way. But always Swami Rastra managed to keep out of reach. Half a dozen times, he was locked in a death grip with a brawny Hindu.

The Spider did not go unscathed in that frenzied mêlée. Those flashing knives took their toll—sliced into his arms and shoulders, grazed his throat time and again, bit deep into his back. He could feel the warm blood running down his ribs, matting against his sleeves. But the wounds served only to drive him on with more grim determination.

These Hindus were only pawns—pawns which he had to eliminate in order to come to grips with Swami Rastra. Irresistibly, he waded through them. Now the golden masked leader was directly in front of him. Wentworth dived for him, clutched at his ornate robe—but Rastra slipped from it and whirled to lash out quickly with his fist. That blow caught Wentworth on his wounded shoulder, sent white-hot agony streaking through his whole side.

Unable to stop himself, he staggered back—and before he could again leap to the attack, the swami was gone! He had disappeared as if by magic!

A trapdoor was the explanation—just as it accounted for the disappearance of the few Hindus who had survived that bloody battle. But Wentworth could not locate it. He was also afraid to tarry there in the sub-cellar for fear it might be a trap that could be flooded with lethal gas. Snatching up one of the knives dropped by the Hindus, he ran to Nita and cut through the transparent oilskin cocoon that enshrouded her. Now he saw that her arms were tightly bound to her sides. Her whole body was wrapped with oil-soaked bandages which would have burned fiercely once the flame reached them. His knife made quick work of this—and then, for a brief moment, she was close in his arms.

"I'm all right, Dick," she whispered, as he released her. "There's another knife. I'll help you with the others."

Feverishly, they worked, liberating the bound captives and setting them to freeing their fellow-victims. The moment they were all released, the Spider led the way out through the door into the passageway he had traversed a few minutes before. Those corridors and stairways were just as he had left them, unobstructed all the way to the cellar of the theater.

"Now you have only one more flight of steps to the street," he whispered to Nita. Then, before she could stop him—before any of those awe-stricken rescued ones had a chance to see what became of him—he had gone back, lone-handed, to follow the trail of Swami Rastra!

THE TORCHES were burning low when he returned to that dungeon charnel house, but they served his purpose. With one in each hand, he searched the floor until he found the outline of a trapdoor in the stone. Then he located the foot-panel, at the rear of Swami Rastra's platform, that released it. The moment he pressed against it, the floor gave way beneath him and slid him down into a stygian tunnel beneath the dungeon.

Again he picked his way carefully along a short corridor and up a flight of steps into a black pit about ten feet square.

At one side the stone ceiling was pierced by an opening perhaps two and a half feet square—a sheer-walled black shaft. But the wall beneath it sloped gently inward and was pitted with several footholds. Wentworth stepped into the first, climbed upward until he was at the ceiling. Then he reached in to grip the metal handholds that had been driven into the shaft's sides. Hand over hand, he worked his way up through the sharply slanting chimney until he reached the trapdoor he expected.

For a moment, he fumbled for the release. Triggering it back, he pulled himself up into a long, narrow compartment about four feet high. Here the floor sloped down sharply from both ends toward the trap in the middle. Again his light picked out a catch in front of him. He opened a panel door and climbed out from behind the back-bar in a fashionable night-club.

The shaft through which he had climbed was a chute that had been used for instantaneously emptying the back-bar of its stock of liquor in the days when the present-day Armageddon Club was a prohibition-era speak-easy!

Now the Armageddon was as quiet as a tomb. Not even a clean-up woman busied herself among the empty, chair-stacked tables. Quietly, Wentworth scouted across the main room to the corridor that led to the offices. He padded up to John Petrillo's private quarters, just as the owner was about to leave with a satchel in his hand.

Petrillo stepped through the doorway—and backed up with a gasp, when an automatic jabbed into his ribs, and the ugly face of the Spider suddenly confronted him.

"Not so fast, Peter Rowland!" the Spider's grating voice

snarled at him. "You have lots of time. The game is up. You have nothing to do but talk, before the police cart you off to jail and start you on your way to the electric chair!"

Petrillo blanched.

"I don't know what you mean!" he sputtered. "I don't know who you are—how you got in here, unless you have come to hold me up. You are too late for that—our receipts all went to the bank last night. I am only here to straighten up my office because the police have closed my club—like all the others."

"That was a very neat trick, Rowland," the Spider grinned like a grimacing gargoyle, "having the police close your place so that you would have a perfect alibi for leaving town to enjoy the millions you have extorted from the society people you have been putting through hell. You might have aroused suspicion, getting out while business was good. But now you are in the clear—or you were until about thirty seconds ago. What have you got in that bag, Rowland—your Swami Rastra outfit, and what else?"

"You must be crazy—I haven't the slightest idea what you are talking about," Petrillo snapped doggedly.

But Wentworth, watching his eyes, saw the desperation flaring in them—the sudden flash of inspiration that blazed there as he stared at the leveled automatic that covered him unwaveringly.

He had suddenly remembered that Wentworth's automatics were empty—that they had been used as clubs downstairs in the dungeon when their last cartridge had been fired! That was the break Petrillo had been wildly seeking!

Wentworth watched his eyes, and knew what Petrillo was going to do—exactly when he would leap back across the office and grab for his own revolver... and Wentworth let him do it.

"So, Mr. Spider—" the man New York night-club patrons knew as John Petrillo panted triumphantly as he glared over the barrel of his leveled gun—"you don't shoot, do you? You can't—because that gun is empty. It's nothing but a bluff. *Drop it!*"

The automatic fell from Wentworth's fingers, thudded on the carpet. Now Petrillo was in front of him, his finger tight on the trigger. He pulled the other empty automatic from its shoulder holster and tossed it aside.

"You are very, very clever, my dear Spider," he grinned exultantly. "So you found out all about me—discovered that I am Peter Rowland and that I was Swami Rastra. It seems too bad that you should have gone to all that trouble. But now it will do you no good. I could not have asked anything more fortunate than to have you pay me this visit. The Spider is the one man I did not want to leave running loose after I left."

He explained. "I have planned and worked too long for this day to have anything arise now and ruin it for me. It has been a long, almost impossible, climb since the day, twelve years ago, when the Crosbys contemptuously paid me off and discarded me. But I started to slave for it the day I cashed their check and put away their dirty money. I dyed my skin and disguised myself as an Italian, so that I could go to work in a speak-easy after that. For two years I stayed there, until my identity was well established. Then I bought into a place myself, with the money they gave me."

He continued: "One place after the other, always bigger and better, higher class so that I would get the 'exclusive' trade I wanted—the trade of the wealthy snobs who made a spectacle of me and cast me out. When I bought the Armageddon, I was just where I wanted to be. All that I needed then was the right moment. That moment came when *The Green Goddess* opened next door, and I learned that the wife who had been too good for me was conducting an affair with Preston Kendall—was meeting him in my place!"

He laughed. "That was all I needed. I knew of the convenient underground passageway connecting this place with the theater. For a man who knows India as I do, Preston Kendall and his stage role were made to order. I saw at once how I could throw suspicion on him and be absolutely safe myself. From that, it was only a step to the plan to revenge myself upon all of New York's society bigwigs by turning their own rotten lives against them."

"That was when you went into partnership with Prince Gooja Singh and organized the crystal-gazers into a racket?"

But Peter Rowland laughed scornfully.

"That faker Gooja Singh—I knew him when he was a swindling guide in Calcutta," he spat. "I used him to put my plan into operation. Now I am going to end it with a bullet through the brain of the Spider, so that the last source of information, that might betray me will be sealed up effectively!"

His finger tightened on the trigger, but again his eyes betrayed him. They contracted ever so slightly as he fired—and in that fraction of a second before the cartridge exploded Richard Wentworth pitched forward, to whip out the Hindu knife he had cached under his garter and flip it with bullet force into Rowland's heart!

TIGHT-LIPPED, HE bent over the still corpse to press his cigarette-lighter against the olive-hued forehead and stamp it with the crimson symbol of inescapable retribution—a grisly warning to all would-be overlords of crime that, even though they might succeed in flouting the constituted authorities, the shadowy, ubiquitous figure of the Spider stood implacably in their path.

More slowly than usual, Wentworth divested himself of the ugly make-up and the Spider's tattered habiliments. He was weakening from loss of blood, but now he would be able to rest—as soon as he had phoned to Stanley Kirkpatrick.

"When you were in trouble you called upon the Spider for help," his discordant voice rasped into the instrument when the police commissioner responded. "Now your crime wave is over—and your man is waiting for you in the office of the Armageddon Club with the proof of his guilt all packed up in a satchel beside him. That makes us quits, Commissioner."

"Wait a minute, Spider," Kirkpatrick begged anxiously. "There are some questions—"

But a wild, cackling laugh jangled in his ear.

"When this case is over, our truce is finished," the Spider reminded—and the click of the receiver was his farewell, his reëntry into the realm of shadows that must forever shroud him.